DISNEY ALADDIN: BOOK OF THE FILM
A CENTUM BOOK 978-1-912841-67-7
Published in Great Britain by Centum Books Ltd
This edition published 2019
1 3 5 7 9 10 8 6 4 2

Centum Books Ltd, 20 Devon Square, Newton Abbot, Devon, TQ12 2HR, UK
books@centumbooksltd.co.uk
CENTUM BOOKS Limited Reg. No. 07641486
A CIP catalogue record for this book is available from the British Library
Printed in United Kingdom

DISNEY

Aladdin

Adapted by Elizabeth Rudnick

Screenplay by John August and Guy Ritchie

Based on Disney's *Aladdin*

Prologue

The mariner stared out at the endless sea before him. If he squinted his eyes and tilted his head just so, he could almost imagine that the waves were dunes of sand, undulating and rippling in the heat of the sun. The squawking of the seagulls hovering above the lone sail that powered his vessel could be, if he listened hard enough, the calls of the camels on the way to market. The sun, though, that was the same—on land or sea.

The mariner sighed. He loved the wildness and freedom of the open ocean. He adored waking at his leisure and doing what he wanted with the day, answering to no one but himself and his family. But he did, at times, miss his home in the sands of the desert.

Hearing an excited shout, the man smiled, the expression brightening his handsome face. The touch of longing disappeared, and he appeared to light up from within. Turning, he looked over at the cause of his happiness. His two children, Lindy and Barro, had come above deck and were leaning over the railing.

"Wow," Lindy said.

"Wow," repeated her younger brother.

Following their gazes, the mariner looked over the railing of his modest ship and saw, in the distance, a not-so-modest ship sailing toward them. It was huge, with many masts boasting brilliantly colored sails. While the sides of the mariner's boat were peeled and in need of a coat of paint, the sides of the other ship were gleaming as if freshly painted that morning. Manning the decks were sailors wearing spotless clothes and, squinting, the mariner could make out elaborate decorations covering the masts and railings.

"Wish ours was that fancy," Barro said with a sigh.

The mariner turned back to his children and raised one eyebrow. "Why? Because it looks better?" He waited for an answer. Getting nothing but shrugs, he went on. "This boat has taken us through many a storm. It might not look like much, but it has something theirs never will. . . ."

"Wood rot and rats?" Barro asked, teasing his father.

The mariner shot his son a look. "Turn around, close your eyes. Now feel how our boat beats with the rhythm of the great unknown. That is its heart. Understand that true value lies deep within." He paused, watching as his two beautiful children listened to his words. At nine and six they were still so young. More than anything, he wanted them to hold on to that innocence. "Now, which ship would you rather have?" he finally asked, when he had given them time to think.

The children's eyes popped open. They glanced at each other. And then, in unison, they answered, "Theirs."

The mariner groaned as the kids began to giggle. Apparently, his lesson had gone unlearned. He needed a new approach. Some way to make his children see how lucky they were to have the waves be their backyard and the ship, their schoolroom. How lucky they were to live each day with grand possibilities and adventure. The mariner narrowed his eyes. How could he get them to see what he wanted them to see?

Then a smile began to tug at his lips. What he

needed was a story. And he happened to know a very good one. "I think it's time I told you the story of Aladdin and the princess and the lamp."

Lindy made a face. "What's so special about a *lamp*?" she asked.

"It's a magic lamp. . . ."

The children exchanged a skeptical look. But then they shrugged. "We're listening," Barro said.

"Well, listen carefully. Because looks can be deceiving. Especially in a place like . . . Agrabah!"

Chapter
One

The sun rose slowly, its light creeping out over the horizon and across the dunes of sand until, at last, it touched the great walls of the city of Agrabah and the brilliant blue sea beyond. Awash in the morning light, the city appeared to glow gold, its fabled bazaars and streets coming to life. The scents of cardamom and other exotic spices filled the air, giving the area a rich perfume all its own. Down at the docks, ships sailed in, their hulls full of treasures from the far reaches of the world. Captains shouted orders to the sailors as they prepared the boats going out to sea, carrying with them all the riches Agrabah had to offer. Above, seabirds circled, their calls as constant as the water lapping on the shore.

In the market, vendors opened their stalls, filling boxes with bright fruits and vegetables, silks and satins, and other exotic treasures they would haggle over and sell when the market opened.

Musicians toting instruments took their places throughout the market, in the shade cast by the large palace that loomed over the entire city. They would soon fill the streets with delightful sounds and, when the day turned to night, bring the citizens of the city out to get lost in the dances and trances of the Arabian night. It was a magical place. A place where it seemed anything was possible and where the streets were full of adventure.

But it wasn't an easy place to make a living. Not for those who called the streets their home. While the palace of Agrabah reflected the region's riches, its streets reflected its reality. To make it, you had to be quick—on your feet and with your wit.

Aladdin stared out at the marketplace. It was quickly growing busy as servants and merchants and townsfolk began to go about their daily business, haggling over prices, looking for the freshest fruit or a special silk. Half a dozen different languages filtered through the air, creating a symphony of sound that was oddly soothing. For Aladdin, the sounds, the people, and the hubbub of the marketplace were as familiar as the back of his own hand. Agrabah had been his home for every day of his twenty years. Born a street rat, he had remained a street rat; the corridors and stalls and alleyways had been his playground, his school. The market was where he had honed his skills at "borrowing" what he needed, when he needed it. He knew that most of those who lived like him had given up hope long ago. They were resigned to a life of just getting by. But not Aladdin. Lifting his eyes to the palace beyond, he felt the same familiar rush he felt every time he took in its towers and caught a hint of the lush gardens beyond. He knew—or rather, he believed—there was more to life. He was going to be somebody—even if that meant just being the best street rat in Agrabah.

Shaking his head, Aladdin began to move through the market. Now was not the time to get lost in daydreams. He had more pressing and real issues—like finding breakfast. As his growling stomach was now reminding him, it had been a day since he had eaten anything and he was in the mood for something sweet. A pomegranate, or maybe a spiced bun from Saja's stall. She always made the best pastries. Just thinking about it made his mouth water. Heading in that direction, he continued planning his day. One thing his less-than-ordinary life required was a plan—and a backup plan to that plan. That morning, he would head to the docks to spot what new goods had arrived in Agrabah with the dawn tide. They would end up in the market the following day, and any street rat worth his salt knew it was best to know what to go after—before anyone else got their hands on it.

On his shoulder, his best friend, a monkey named Abu, chattered away. Nodding absently in reply as the monkey let out a particularly shrill set of screeches, Aladdin nearly bumped into a woman. Startled, he took a step back. But then a large smile spread across his face as he took in the brilliant—and clearly very expensive—jewel at her throat.

"What's your monkey's name?" the woman asked.

"Abu," Aladdin said. In response, Abu tipped the small fez he wore on his head and scampered from Aladdin's shoulder to the woman's arm.

The woman let out a delighted laugh. "He's a lovely monkey," she said, cooing to Abu as he weaved around her shoulders.

Aladdin shot the monkey a look. Abu nodded and continued to scamper, faster and faster. Then, turning his attention back to the woman, Aladdin nodded at her neck. "And that's a lovely necklace," he pointed out.

Reaching a hand to her throat, the woman touched the bright jewel hanging off the thick chain around her neck. Aladdin's eyes followed her fingers, but his ears stayed tuned to the noises around him. He had been on the streets long enough to know when he was being conned. And beautiful, beguiling women didn't just walk up to young street rats without some intention—and it was usually not a good intention. Sure enough, he heard a rustle and then felt the slightest of tugs on the bag he carried over his shoulder.

Quick as a wink, Aladdin reached over his shoulder, grabbing a thin, smooth hand just as it reached into his bag. Pulling the hand forward, he found himself face-to-face with another young woman, clearly the accomplice. He knew this routine. Distract and snatch. "Hello," he said, flashing one of his most charming smiles, which lit up his face and made him still more handsome. "I think that belongs to me. Should've gone for the pocket, but you had to go for the bag. Greed . . . it'll get you every time."

The woman who had initially caught Aladdin's attention shrugged. "Didn't have anything worth stealing anyway," she said. Turning, the two slunk off into the crowds of the market. Aladdin could hear them grumbling and knew they were already looking for their next mark.

After all, that was what he would have been doing.

Quickly, Aladdin shimmied up the rough wall of a nearby building. Jumping over onto the roof, he waited for Abu to join him. "How'd we do?" he asked the monkey.

In answer, Abu ran up onto Aladdin's shoulder and held out his tiny hand. Clutched in it was the necklace the woman had been wearing. "Good monkey," Aladdin said, pleased. He knew that he looked the part of an easy con. He was anything but. Lifting the necklace so it caught the sun and sparkled enticingly, Aladdin smiled more broadly. And now he was a street rat who was that much richer.

Chapter

Two

D alia stood, arms crossed, waiting. On the other side of the elaborate doors to her mistress's chambers, she could hear the heavy footsteps of the palace guards coming closer. She could also hear Jasmine's protests as the princess tried to talk her way out of her current situation.

A moment later, the doors swung open, revealing Jasmine. The princess attempted to retain some dignity as she was unceremoniously shown inside, and the doors slammed shut behind her. Dalia tried not to smile.

"How far did you make it this time?" Dalia asked.

Jasmine raised one perfectly arched eyebrow. "I thought I saw a gate they missed," she said. She began to pace around her chambers. More library than bedroom, her chambers' walls were covered in maps, and books lined the shelves and toppled over on tables and chairs. Lush, thick curtains framed tall windows that looked out over the city—*her* city—below.

Dalia followed behind Jasmine, her voice growing gentle. She knew how desperately Jasmine longed to see more than the walls of the palace. But Dalia also knew what Jasmine did deep down—that Jasmine was the princess of Agrabah. And as such, her place seemed to be *behind* the walls. "Don't worry, one day you'll escape," she said, trying to sound positive.

Jasmine let out a sigh. "How can I lead a people I don't even know?" she asked. Walking toward a window, she looked out into the courtyard. The trees nearest the window had all been trimmed so that Jasmine could not attempt to climb down them (again). A guard stood at attention in the garden below, and the windows lower to the ground had been barred. All reactions to Jasmine's frequent attempts to escape.

"No one is asking you to," Dalia pointed out. "All you have to do is wake up and act like a princess and wait for death."

"As enticing as that sounds," Jasmine replied, raising an eyebrow at her friend's poor attempt at humor, "I want more than that. I want to be with the people of Agrabah." She walked the rest of the way to the window and flopped down on the large window seat. Raja, her beloved tiger, padded up and placed his large head in Jasmine's lap. Absently, Jasmine began to pat the creature's beautiful head. She had had the tiger since Raja was a cub. The animal's large size, huge paws, and sharp teeth were practically unnoticeable to Jasmine. All she saw was a friend and companion, one constant in the palace life around her. The other constant? Her desire to go beyond the palace walls.

Her world was limited—her opulent chambers, the garden with its plants and animals placed to make it feel as though the environs were natural. But like her happiness in her home, it was all a facade. The garden was nothing more than pretend, and most of the time, Jasmine felt that she, too, was pretending. Pretending to love her life, pretending to care about her silly day-to-day tasks. She sighed. No. She wasn't happy spending her days reading about other people living their lives to the fullest, sultans risking it all for their people. She wanted to be living those things herself, *doing* them herself. "Tell me again about the market," she finally said, gazing over at her handmaiden.

Dalia smiled gently. She loved Jasmine like a sister. They were, in many ways, as close as sisters. Dalia had been a part of Jasmine's life for as long as the princess could remember. And as such, there were times, even though Jasmine was the princess and Dalia the handmaiden, that Dalia wished she could ignore Jasmine's requests. Especially when it was the same request she had heard countless times before. "Remember the time you wanted to see where I live?" Dalia said. Jasmine nodded. "Then, when you saw it you screamed, and then you were sad?" Dalia continued.

Jasmine frowned and shook her head. That was *not* how it had happened. Not exactly, at least. There *may* have been some tears, but she was pretty sure that was just because she stubbed her toe, not because seeing where Dalia lived made her sad.

Ignoring the princess's look, Dalia went on. "The market is exactly like that," she said. "Why would you want to go there?"

Getting to her feet, Jasmine began to walk around her chambers, her fingers brushing along the myriad of maps that lined the walls. Some were ancient, their edges frayed and their writing faded. Others were newer, marking territory claimed by Agrabah during Jasmine's twenty years. Old or new, Jasmine loved them all. But maps weren't enough anymore. She wanted to be more than just an observer of her country and her people. She just needed to convince her father. "I know these maps better than I know my own city," she said softly. "Help me sneak out, Dalia. If I can prove to Baba that I have the knowledge and experience to lead, he might change his mind. And I'll never learn any of that stuck in a palace." Her words bounced around the chamber and Jasmine could hear the desperation in her own voice.

Dalia shook her head. "If you get caught, I'll be thrown in the dungeon."

"You know I'd never let anything happen to you," Jasmine said.

"The dungeon," Dalia repeated. "That is the thing that would be happening to me."

It was time to change tactics. Walking over to her, Jasmine took her handmaiden's hands in her own and gave her the most pathetic expression it seemed she could muster. Dalia was a softy deep down. Jasmine just needed to pull on the right heartstring. "Any moment now, I'll end up married to some puffed-up prince and I may never get this chance again," the princess continued. The thought of being shackled to someone she didn't love did in fact make Jasmine's heart ache and her eyes water. "Please, Dalia?"

Dalia sighed. Then slowly, she began to nod. "I hate that I'm weak and can be talked into anything and can't say no," she said, trying not to smile.

But Jasmine wasn't listening. The princess had let out an excited squeal and was clapping her hands together happily. Then she threw her arms around her best friend.

"I wish I didn't love you," Dalia said.

Jasmine just squeezed harder. Wishes weren't real. But going to see the market? That was finally, *really* happening.

Jasmine nervously pulled at the hem of her cloak, wishing she hadn't been so quick to brush off Dalia's offer to accompany her. It would have been comforting to know where she was going. But as she made her way deeper into the market, she soon forgot to be nervous, instead growing enchanted by the multitude of new smells, sounds, and sights. She had read so much about her own city and now it was coming to life in front of her very eyes. She wanted to squeal with excitement but quickly thought better of it.

Everything seemed brighter, Jasmine thought as she walked through the stalls. The palace was beautiful and opulent, but it was muted. The windows filtered the full strength of the sun, and the thick walls meant to keep out the heat of the day also kept out the smells. Here nothing was muted. She passed among the stalls, her eyes growing wide as she took in purple eggplants and yellow bananas, green melons and glistening oranges lined up to tantalize passersby. More stalls were filled with spices from around the world, their scents pungent and unfamiliar. Lifting a hand, Jasmine ran a finger over a row of rugs. She smiled as her eyes wandered over an intricate pattern on red-and-yellow fabric, the shot of blue throughout reminding her of Agrabah itself and its proximity to the sea. It was no wonder people who came to Agrabah were instantly enchanted. She had lived there her whole life and yet felt like she was seeing this city of rainbow colors for the first time.

Catching sight of a particularly beautiful piece of pottery, Jasmine headed toward the other side of the market. She let out a startled cry as she nearly tripped over a young child hunched on the ground, picking at the meager crumbs of bread that had fallen from a cart. Her eyes welled with tears as she took in the boy's protruding ribs and the fevered way he shoved morsels of food into his mouth, as though he hadn't eaten in days.

She was so focused on him she didn't register the handsome man standing nearby, juggling apples and teasing the fruit vendor. Nor did she bother to notice that the vendor, while ignoring the juggling man, was eyeing her warily. Concealed beneath the cloak of her borrowed servant's uniform, she only had eyes for the boy and the girl who had joined him, also making a meal from crumbs.

Reaching up, Jasmine pulled two loaves of bread from the nearby stall and handed them to the children. "There you go . . ." she said.

The children didn't hesitate. Grabbing the loaves, they shoved them under their arms and took off. Suddenly, there was a shout from the next stall. Looking over, she saw that the owner was staring at her angrily. His fists were clenched. "You steal from my brother!" he cried.

Jasmine gulped. This was exactly what Dalia had warned her *not* to do. "Don't draw any attention to yourself, Princess," she had said while trying to answer Jasmine's endless questions about what to expect beyond the gates. Jasmine's love of learning extended beyond just maps. Finding out as much as she could about her city before she went out into it felt natural—even if it drove Dalia slightly crazy. "Keep your head down. Look all you want but do *not* touch. The last thing you want is someone noticing you."

Unfortunately, someone was definitely noticing her now.

Holding up her hands, Jasmine tried to placate the vendor. "Stealing, no sir," she began. "I don't know your brother—" She was cut short as the man grabbed her by the arm and pushed back the long sleeve of her cloak. The gold from the bracelet she had forgotten to take off glimmered in the sun.

"Stop!" she said with as much authority as she could muster, struggling in the man's tightening grip. Her heart was pounding against her chest. If he pulled off her cloak, he might discover who she really was. And if that happened, her father would find out and she might not get another chance to see everything that lay beyond the palace walls.

"Take it easy, Jamal, that's no way to treat a lady."

The kind voice startled Jasmine and she turned, wrenching her arm free. A young man stood near her, his dark brown eyes curious and calm despite the anger radiating from Jamal. Behind him, Jasmine could see several members of the city guard pushing their way through the growing crowd of people.

"Keep your street-rat nose out of it!" Jamal shouted. Clearly, the two knew each other.

As Jasmine watched, a small monkey scampered up the young man's arm and made to attack Jamal. But the man pulled the monkey's tail, shaking his head no. Then he turned and looked directly at Jasmine. For a split second, she forgot to breathe. There was something in his eyes, a kindness and a mysteriousness—and determination. He was a young man, but his eyes were wise with experience.

Coming closer, he lowered his head and

whispered into her ear, "Do you have any money?" When she shook her head, his brows furrowed. "Okay," he finally said. "Do you trust me?"

Jasmine looked up, surprised. Trust him? She had only just met him. Yet there really wasn't much of a choice. If she didn't take his help, she was likely to lose her bracelet—or worse, be found out, and potentially be given more limitations than she already had. She nodded.

Still gazing into her eyes, the young man reached out and slipped the bracelet off her wrist. Turning, he held it out to Jamal. The man snatched it from him and then raised it to his mouth, biting the gold to make sure it was real.

"It's what you wanted, right?" the young man asked. Jamal nodded. "Good. And an apple for your troubles?" The young man handed an apple over. The transaction complete, the young man took Jasmine by the arm and began to steer her away from the stall. But not before he plucked up the bracelet, which Jamal had only moments ago put down, and replaced it with one of the apples he'd been juggling. When they were a few steps away, the young man leaned over and whispered to

Jasmine so quietly that she almost missed it: "Get ready to run."

Run? Jasmine's eyes grew wider and once again her heart began to race. Was he serious?

As if on cue, Jamal, realizing what had really just happened, let out an angry shout. Immediately, the guards, who had slowed their pace when it looked like things had been settled peacefully, broke into a sprint.

"Down that alley!" the young man shouted as Jasmine looked frantically between the guards and him. "Monkey knows the way." The small furry creature jumped off his shoulder and onto hers. Then the young man swiftly climbed up onto a table in the market and began to wave his hands in the air. The jewelry he had taken back from Jamal glimmered and shone in the bright sunlight.

Jasmine stood, rooted to the dusty ground at her feet, until the young man told her to run once more. She didn't need to be told again. She took off, hearing the loud, pounding footsteps of the guards behind her.

Unfortunately, while she was able to run, she wasn't sure exactly where she was running *to*, and the little monkey was now nowhere to be seen.

The man hadn't told her anything but "Down that alley," and that alley happened to have some twists and turns. Taking a wild guess, she went right and then left and then, finally, the alley straightened out. After hearing a series of exclamations—"Ow!" "Watch it!"—she wasn't surprised when, a moment later, the young man—and the monkey—turned the corner and appeared in front of her. He stopped suddenly, and for a long moment, he just stared at her. Then, grabbing her hand, he pulled her back down the alley the way they had come.

Chapter

Three

As Aladdin ran through the streets he pumped a triumphant fist in the air. That had been close—or at least closer than he liked to play it. But he usually acted alone during a con. At most he had Abu, and Abu was almost an extension of himself. He had never had to outwit Jamal before with a strange servant girl tagging along. Well, not so much tagging along as sort of getting in the way. But he had done it nevertheless. His smile grew broader as he thought back to Jamal's look of disbelief when he saw the bracelet was gone.

Aladdin's footsteps slowed as he turned down the alley and saw the servant girl waiting for him. He hadn't been thinking when he'd stepped in between her and Jamal. It had sort of just . . . happened. While he hadn't been able to clearly see the girl's face hidden beneath her cloak, he had seen her hands flutter at the sound of Jamal's angry voice and had been compelled to help. She was clearly not used to the market or to the children who made it their job to beg for scraps among the stalls. But despite that, she had remained composed during the whole thing, her back straight, her head held high. And never once had she tried to give the children up. She had let them go with their bread, even at the cost of her bracelet. It was rare for someone to be kind to the children who made their homes on the street, and a part of Aladdin wondered what it would have been like if someone had done that for him. It had seemed wrong to turn his back on the girl—plus, he did like a good chase. Kept him in shape.

The cloak slid from the girl's head, revealing her face.

And Aladdin nearly stopped breathing.

The servant girl was by far the most beautiful woman he had ever seen. Her long, dark hair cascaded down her shoulders and her back in thick waves. Her eyes were a deep chestnut color, and her skin seemed to glow from within.

Dragging his attention from the vision before him, Aladdin heard the guards getting closer. They had to keep moving. Reaching out, he grabbed hold of her hand and began to walk swiftly down the alley.

"I wasn't stealing, just to clarify," the girl said a little breathlessly. "Those children were hungry, and he had bread, so I simply—"

"That's called stealing," Aladdin pointed out, cutting her off. "And if they catch you, you'll spend the next three weeks in the stocks!" As they burst out of the alley and into one of the many smaller squares that dotted Agrabah, Aladdin nodded toward a man whose head and arms were sticking out from between two pieces of rough-hewn wood. "How you getting along there, Omar?"

The young woman grew pale at the sight of Omar. Aladdin was genuinely surprised. She seemed very sheltered from the harsher realities of life on the streets of Agrabah. And the bracelet? What servant girl would wear such an expensive piece of jewelry—especially into the market? Something wasn't adding up, but he couldn't put a finger on it. Not yet, at least. As if aware of his thoughts, the girl asked, "How much trouble are we in?" The naiveté of her question made Aladdin's suspicions grow.

"You're only in trouble if you get caught!" Aladdin answered wryly. Then, as the guards' shouts echoed behind them, and before the girl could mutter even a word of protest, Aladdin grabbed her hand and began to sprint.

He had been keeping one step ahead of guards his entire life. It was what he had to do. Like the children the girl had given bread to, he had stood in lines, waiting for handouts. He had stolen, not because he enjoyed it, but because he couldn't afford *not* to steal. He knew the logic was convoluted and people would argue there were other ways to make a life in Agrabah, but he didn't mind it—usually. He always seemed to make it work. Others, unfortunately, were not so lucky, and though he tried to share his wares with those who needed it, he wished he could do more to help.

Like this servant girl had done with the children and the bread.

Rushing up a flight of stairs, then down another, Aladdin paused at the opening of a tunnel he had used as an escape in the past. He glanced quickly behind him. The servant girl was doing her best to keep up, but she was still struggling. A long, dark tunnel would probably just slow them down. And the number one rule when running was *not* to slow down. Come to think of it, that was also rule two and rule three. Thinking fast, Aladdin knocked on a door as they ran past. A moment later, someone opened it. There was a loud thunk followed by a string of muttered grunts as the guards ran right into the door and fell to the ground.

Aladdin let out a happy shout but kept running. He knew the guards would be back on their feet and after him in no time. That was rule four. Stay ahead of the laymen. They had no patience nor appreciation for the talents of a street rat. Which was ironic, Aladdin couldn't help thinking as he and the servant girl raced out of an alley into one of the main tanneries of Agrabah. Most of the guards had gotten their start on the streets.

"Riffraff!"

Hearing the angry shout, Aladdin jumped up onto a thin walkway that ran over the tannery vats. He and the girl deftly and easily made their way over the huge tubs full of different colors of dye. The guards were not as lucky. They fell, one by one, into the vats, emerging with another round of muttered—and now even more colorful—curses.

"Take that!" Aladdin shouted. He was enjoying

himself, minus the name-calling. He was managing to stay ahead of the guards and keep the servant girl safe. In his mind, that was win-win. Rounding yet another corner, he steered the girl through a door and then doubled back, heading toward a cart that was tipped forward and resting precariously on its handles. He quickly grabbed a heavy bag that was lying nearby and then balanced himself on the cart's handles. Just as the guards approached, he heaved the bag into the opposite end of the cart and sent himself flying into the air and onto the safety of the nearby rooftop.

Letting out a deep breath—he hadn't been *completely* sure that would work—he once again began to run, only this time he leapt from rooftop to rooftop, hearing Abu skitter nearby. Aladdin scanned the windows below and waited until he spotted the one he knew best. Smiling, he took a deep breath and jumped—right through the window!

He heard shrieks and smelled perfume, but Aladdin couldn't see anything. He was blinded by bright, flowing fabric that swirled and twirled about him in a dizzying display. Then he heard a familiar woman's voice shout out his name amid a round of giggles. As planned, he had crashed right into a window of Agrabah's school for girls. He smiled, pulling a piece of fabric away from his eyes. Taking a deep bow, and receiving another round of giggles, he jumped back out the window and proceeded to bounce from one shop awning to the next, all the way back down to the street.

He crashed to the ground, letting out a groan, just as the cloaked servant girl appeared in the doorway. "There are stairs, you know!" she said, shaking her head at Aladdin's disheveled appearance and ragged breathing.

He shrugged, getting to his feet. "But where's the fun in that?" he asked.

Not waiting for an answer, Aladdin once more took the girl's hand and continued on. But no matter where Aladdin led them—down alleyways or up to the rooftops—or how slyly he maneuvered, the guards stayed pretty close behind.

Reaching the top of a particularly high roof, Aladdin slid to a stop. The drop between roofs was now at least forty feet, and the gap between the two buildings was too far to jump without some assistance. Looking behind him, he saw the guards closing in. He glanced at the concerned expression on the girl's face.

And then he saw a long pole. His eyes narrowed thoughtfully. It was a long shot, but if the girl was up for it, they had their out right there. Realizing what he wanted her to do, the girl's mouth dropped open. "We jump?" she asked.

He nodded. Handing her the pole, he turned and leapt across to the other side. Once there, he whipped back around — and waited.

But the girl didn't move. She just kept looking down at the ground. "It's a long way down," she said, the pole shaking in her hands. She began to back away.

Seeing the doubt in her eyes, Aladdin tried to focus her attention. "Look at me," he said. "Look at me." When she finally dragged her gaze to meet his, he smiled. "You can do it!"

Taking a deep breath, she backed up as far as she could. Then she took off running. Just before the roof ended, she planted the pole, flinging herself over the gap and landing on the roof beyond. She looked over at Aladdin, surprise and pride filling her face.

He breathed a sigh of relief.

Then Aladdin grabbed an old rolled-up rug that someone had left to rot on the roof. He walked over to the edge of the building and began to swing it back and forth. When he had enough momentum, he let go of the rug. It sailed out of his hands—and right through a window several stories down, smashing the glass into pieces. When the guards arrived, they would think Aladdin had crashed through and go after him.

But they wouldn't find him. Because he had no intention of being anywhere near there when they came. "I know somewhere we'll be safe," he told the girl as the monkey rejoined them and hurried onto Aladdin's shoulder. "Come with me."

Jasmine had never been more exhausted—or elated—in her whole life. She couldn't believe what she had just done. Run from guards? Leapt over forty-foot drops? Trusted a boy she didn't even know? But somehow, it had all just seemed right. Like it had been meant to happen.

And now she was following this stranger into an old tower that looked like it was about to fall down any minute.

"Where are we exactly?" she asked.

"You'll see," the young man replied. Reaching

up, he pulled on a hidden rope. A set of wooden stairs appeared. Gesturing for her to follow, he began to climb up.

Despite their decrepit appearance, the steps were surprisingly solid. Her mind racing with curiosity, Jasmine ascended toward the unknown. A few flights up, the stairs ended, and the young man disappeared through a rough doorway. Jasmine followed.

As she walked through the door, her breath caught in her throat. There, in front of her, displayed like one of the paintings in the palace—but *better*—was the city of Agrabah. One whole wall of the tower had fallen away, resulting in a wide-open expanse. Jasmine had spent her entire life surrounded by the most beautiful things money and royalty could buy, yet she had never seen anything as perfect or breathtaking as the view of Agrabah from this secret beggar's hideaway.

Her smile faded as she saw, in the distance, the guards still on the hunt. Their number seemed to have increased and she couldn't help wondering why so many were needed for what was really a simple misunderstanding. It seemed unnecessary—as was the way in which they were so quick to pull their swords, frightening those in their path. It was a side of Agrabah she had never thought existed, and it saddened her to know now that it did. She had a feeling a certain vizier must be behind it all.

"Abu. Make our guest some tea," the young man said, startling Jasmine. She looked over and saw that he was addressing the monkey. A monkey who, apparently, was not pleased with the request. He shot the young man a look and began to chatter to himself angrily.

"I can't believe . . ." Jasmine's voice faded. She wasn't sure why she had started to speak her thoughts out loud.

"What?" the young man pressed. His big, warm eyes looked at her in a way she had never been looked at before. Like he *wanted* to hear what she had to say next.

She walked closer to the open wall of the tower. For some reason, she felt comfortable telling this stranger what she was thinking. He was easy to talk to. "I can't believe we did that," she said. "That *I* did that . . . that we're alive." She stopped, catching sight of the amused expression on the stranger's face. Her cheeks flushed self-consciously. She had wanted to get outside the palace walls because she had wanted to see what life was really like for her people. She realized, staring around at this man's home—without the comforts she took for granted in the palace . . . without *walls* even—that he probably had to do what they had just done more often than not. "Thank you for getting me out of there." She stopped at that, at a loss for anything else to say.

"You're welcome." The young man cocked his head. "I'm Aladdin. And your name is?"

Jasmine hesitated. She was sure there were plenty of Jasmines in Agrabah who were *not* the princess, but she didn't want to risk it. "Dalia," she said, thinking quickly. Her handmaiden wouldn't mind if she borrowed her identity temporarily.

"Dalia," Aladdin said, giving her another charming smile. "The talented thief . . . from the palace."

Jasmine froze at his words. How had he known she was from the palace? How *could* he know? She had done everything Dalia had told her to do. Well, almost everything. Minus the whole unfortunate bread incident . . . She opened and closed her mouth, not sure what to do or say next.

"Only someone from the palace could afford a bracelet like that," Aladdin went on. "We know you didn't steal it."

The breath whooshed from Jasmine's lungs. He *didn't* know. At least, he didn't know the most important part. She tried to calm her pounding heart as he continued revealing how he had deduced where she came from.

He looked her over, raising an eyebrow. "You smell good—spiced amber that isn't from around here. That silk lining is imported, too. Those come off the merchant boats and only go to the palace. But not to servants . . ." His voice trailed off and his eyes narrowed.

Jasmine's heart, which had finally begun to slow, started racing once more. This was it. He really had discovered her secret. She should run. But she honestly didn't know where to go.

Unaware of her building panic, Aladdin finished his observations. "At least, not *most* servants." He paused, and Jasmine realized that only now had he figured out who she was. Everything he had said to this point was his way of talking it out. She braced herself.

"So you must be a handmaid to the princess, right?"

Chapter

Four

Oh, I am good, Aladdin thought as he stared at the beautiful servant girl in front of him. He had just figured her out with nothing to go on but her clothes, a fancy bracelet, and some keen observations.

Turning away from her, he walked to the window of his broken tower and looked out at Agrabah. He had been living there, tucked above the city, for years. But Dalia was the first person he had ever brought to his home. It had felt right, somehow, to bring her there, and while he knew Abu wasn't happy—the monkey was still chattering away—Aladdin was glad to be spending time with her. He wanted to get to know her better, to understand why she would leave the palace in the first place.

Looking back at Dalia, he gestured at the colorful landscape outside the window. "You should tell the princess she should get out more," he said.

"She needs to see what the guards are doing to the city."

To his surprise, Dalia looked visibly upset by his words. Her eyes grew sad and she clasped her hands, her knuckles turning pale. "They won't let her. Ever since m—" She stopped, shaking her head. "Ever since the Queen was killed, the Sultan's been afraid. And his vizier preys on his fear."

Aladdin nodded. Everyone had been afraid since the Queen had been killed. Stumbling upon a group of vicious thieves while making her way through the market, she had been attacked and left for dead. Before then, the Sultan and the Queen had often found their way down to walk among their people. They had been beloved by the citizens of Agrabah. The Queen's kindness and beauty were spoken of throughout the city, the Sultan's benevolence known and trusted.

But the Queen's death had changed all that. "Those thieves weren't even from Agrabah," Aladdin said softly. "The people loved her."

"They did, didn't they," the servant girl said, her own voice soft. Nervously, she began to walk around the hideaway, running her fingers over odds and ends that Aladdin and Abu had "collected" together over the years. Knocking over a stringed instrument, Dalia looked up guiltily. "I'm sorry." Leaning down, she picked it up and held it in her hands. She began to strum. The music bounced off the walls and covered them both in a blanket of sound. Aladdin watched, mesmerized by the way her fingers effortlessly moved over the strings, the way the instrument seemed an extension of her arms. Aladdin realized he was humming along to the tune.

As the music faded, Aladdin smiled at Dalia. "My mother taught me that song," he said, fondness in his voice.

"Mine too," Dalia said, looking surprised by his revelation. "It's all I remember of her." She paused wistfully, then turned back to him. "And . . . your father?"

"I lost them both when I was young," Aladdin said. "Been on my own ever since." He felt his throat close with emotions he had pushed down for a long, long time. Fighting to regain control of himself and the moment, he shook his head. "But it's not so bad. I've got a monkey." Hearing Aladdin, Abu finally stopped chattering angrily and looked up, clearly pleased to be what made his friend happy. "I just put one foot in front of the other and get through the day. Only . . ."

He let his voice trail off. Should he share how he truly felt? What he really longed for? Dalia seemed to be interested, and she hadn't run screaming from him yet. But so far he had been playing it pretty cool. . . .

"What?" Dalia prompted.

Aladdin shrugged. Why not tell her? He would honestly probably never see her again, and he couldn't deny there was something about her that tugged at him, made him wish he were a different person. "I wake up every day wishing things will be different," he finally said. "But it never seems to change. Sometimes, I almost feel—"

"Trapped."

Aladdin's head snapped up. He looked over at the servant girl. That was exactly what he had been about to say.

She went on, her words echoing the ones in his head. "Like you can't escape what you were born into . . ."

Their eyes locked and silence fell over the tower. Aladdin felt something rush through him. Something he hadn't allowed himself to feel since his parents had died, something he couldn't quite name yet but knew with certainty he wanted to feel again. He felt his arm begin to reach for Dalia's, his fingers tingling at the anticipation of touching her hand—

And then a loud trumpeting sound blasted through the air, startling them both. Looking out through the opening in the tower wall, they saw a fleet of ships entering the harbor. The trumpets sounded again, announcing the arrival of someone important.

"I have to get back to the palace," Dalia said, her expression hardening, the moment between them lost.

Aladdin nodded. He was sure that whomever it was who had just sailed into the harbor was heading to the palace. And that meant Dalia would most likely have to get back and help her princess prepare for the visitors. Ushering her down the stairs, Aladdin led her in the direction of the palace. They saw a procession begin to form at the docks, and Dalia's footsteps quickened as Aladdin rushed to keep up.

"Another prince coming to court the princess . . ." he speculated.

"Yes. And I have to get—" The girl stopped and looked confused for a moment, then shook her head. "*Her* ready. Do you have my bracelet?"

Nodding, Aladdin reached into the bag he always carried across his chest. Small but deep, it was a great place to put things he picked up during the day. "Sure, it's right—" He stopped. He dug his hand deeper and rummaged around, his brow furrowing. "I'm sure I put it in here. . . ."

Next to him, Dalia frowned as she watched him struggle. He knew what she was thinking. It was written all over her face. "That was my mother's bracelet," she said, her eyes dark with fury. "You *are* a thief. I'm so naive!"

"No!" Aladdin protested. "It's not like that—"

But Dalia didn't wait to hear his excuse. She disappeared into the growing crowd that was gathering to see the newest prince to arrive in Agrabah. In seconds, she had blended in among the people and vanished.

Aladdin stood looking into the crowd with a mixture of hope and frustration. Hope that Dalia would come back, and frustration that she had left thinking he was a thief. Which, while technically true, wasn't true in *this* case. He honestly had no idea where the bracelet had gone. He was just about to go after her when he was almost run off the street by a line of drummers. They banged on their instruments, heralding the presence of one Prince Anders of Skånland.

Jumping back to safety, Aladdin saw that not everyone was as quick on their feet. Two small children were frozen in fear—right in the path of the giant horses carrying the palace guards. Aladdin looked desperately back and forth between the guards and the children, hoping the guards would see the little ones and pull their mounts up. But the guards were oblivious to anything but the prince they were protecting.

Aladdin groaned. He was going to have to do something. He couldn't just watch the children get flattened. Leaping forward, he put himself between the lead guard's horse and the two small children. The horse let out a fierce whinny and reared back on its hind legs, its powerful legs kicking at the air. On the horse's back, the guard let out an angry shout.

"Street rat! Get out of the way!"

"Who are you calling a—" The words were out

of Aladdin's mouth before he could stop himself. He clamped his mouth shut, but it was too late.

In a group, the guards dismounted and surrounded him, pushing him back against a wall. At that very moment, someone threw a bucket of slop out a window a few stories up. It fell all over Aladdin, covering him in kitchen refuse.

The guard whose horse had reared let out a cruel laugh. Jabbing his finger against Aladdin's chest, he shook his head. "You were born insignificant, you'll die insignificant, and only your fleas will mourn you," he said. Then, with a sneer, he got back on his horse and the procession continued.

As the crowd dispersed, Aladdin brushed an orange peel off his shoulder and let out a sigh. What good was it to help others? It had gotten him nowhere today. He had made Dalia mad and gotten a leftover-soup shower trying to help the kids. Maybe the guard was right. Maybe he was just a street rat and always would be. But, he thought as he headed back to his tower, he wanted to be so much more. He wanted Dalia to see that he *was* so much more.

He climbed up the steps and walked over to

look out at the palace, his mind still swirling. He wanted Dalia, and everyone, to know that if they only took the time to look closer, they would see he wasn't just a thief. But how could that ever happen if no one took a chance on him? How could he prove himself to Dalia when he would probably never see her again?

Feeling a tug on the bottom of his pants, he looked down and saw Abu. The little monkey's familiar face at least made Aladdin smile. The monkey scampered up and stopped on his shoulder, chattering excitedly. Then he reached under the small vest he wore and pulled out a piece of jewelry. Aladdin's eyes narrowed. It wasn't just any piece of jewelry; it was the bracelet Dalia had been wearing.

"Abu!" Aladdin shouted. "Now she thinks I'm a thief!"

The monkey shrugged as if to say, *And your point?*

"I mean, she thinks I stole *from her*," he said.

Grabbing the bracelet out of Abu's hand, Aladdin walked over to the gaping hole in the tower. In the distance, the palace was afire with the setting sun and candles in the windows as everyone prepared for the arrival of Prince Anders.

A smile spread across Aladdin's face. That was it. Everyone was waiting for Prince Anders—which meant everyone would be distracted. Which *meant* it would be a very good time to try to sneak in and find a certain princess's handmaiden and return her bracelet. . . .

Chapter
Five

Jasmine was late. She had managed to sneak back into the palace as fast as she could and hadn't even had a chance to fill Dalia in on her adventure—and missing bracelet—before another servant had come to tell her that her presence was requested in the Great Hall.

Racing from her chambers, Jasmine couldn't help comparing the luxurious walls of the palace with the streets she had been wandering less than an hour before. They were in such close proximity, yet so different. *Just like Aladdin and I,* she thought, surprised by the way her heart hitched at the thought of his name. Stopping in front of the huge doors that led into the Great Hall, Jasmine could hear the voice of her father.

"Welcome, Prince Anders!" the Sultan said. "We trust you had an enjoyable journey?"

"Ja," another voice answered in a thick accent.

"Our ships are such good design, we barely feel the waves. It's like you are on clouds or something—"

Jasmine took a deep breath. She loved her father and knew he was probably hating every minute of the small talk. He had always left that to her mother, and without her there, he was lost. Smoothing her hands against the rich, soft fabric of her gown—a deep pink the color of a vibrant sunrise, complete with a long train that slowed her pace more than she liked—she pushed open the door and walked out onto the landing beyond. She stood for a moment, looking down the length of the golden stairs to the men gathered at the bottom. As the door shut behind her, the noise echoing through the Great Hall, everyone looked up. She saw her father's warm smile and kind eyes, a comfort as she found herself once again on display. Holding her head up, she began to walk down the long stairs, feeling Prince Anders's appreciative gaze on her. Despite the layers of elegant clothing, she shivered, moving more slowly than she would have liked due to the long train trailing behind her. At her side, Raja purred deeply, his presence comforting—and protective.

As she reached the bottom of the stairs, her

dress flowing out behind her, she caught Prince Anders's approving nod. Clearly, the dress Dalia had chosen had done the trick—at least insomuch as it was supposed to wow the prince speechless. But Jasmine couldn't help wondering what he must be thinking. From all she had read, his homeland was simple and sparse—colored by earthy tones, dominated by woods and snow. The hardworking people made do with small pleasures and rough homes, content to live off the land and enjoy the natural beauty. But as she lifted her eyes and took another look at Prince Anders's formal attire, clearly made of rich fabric, she remembered she had also read that the royal family did not live quite so simply. In fact, it was said that while they were content to let their people live meager lives, the royal family enjoyed life in excess. Opulent palaces, huge feasts to mark any day of even minor import, and a queen who enjoyed jewels—any and all shapes, sizes, and colors. Jasmine couldn't help wondering if the people of Agrabah would say the same of their royal family. Did they think she and her father were that out of touch?

The thought made Jasmine sigh, wishing for the millionth time that she could have a more active role in leading Agrabah—even more so as she made her way deeper into the Great Hall. The room literally sparkled. Every surface, from the pillars to the walls, was covered in intricate gold. Exotic birds, the same that wandered the gardens outside, were carved into the stairs and on the walls. Fish swam up the pillars in abundance, as they did in the sea beyond. When Jasmine had been a girl, she had spent hours staring at the birds—their wings spread—wondering what it would be like to just be able to fly away. To see the world from above, not be stuck in one place. She sighed. All that wondering had gotten her nowhere. Like the fish etched in gold, she was stuck in her place. And probably would be always.

Jasmine noticed that her father's head guard, Hakim, was there as always, protecting the Sultan. She tried not to groan when she spotted Jafar, the palace vizier, along with his annoying parrot, Iago. She felt the vizier's eyes on her and shivered in disgust. She had never liked the man and disliked him even more now that he had ingratiated himself into her father's life. Since her mother's death, the man had been omnipresent, his words and opinions the only things her father seemed to hear.

Finally arriving at the end of the hall, Jasmine leaned down and gave her father a kiss on the cheek. Then she straightened up and turned toward the visiting prince.

"Prince Anders," the Sultan said, "my daughter, Princess Jasmine."

Bowing her head, Jasmine reluctantly held out her hand so the prince could, as was custom, raise it to his lips. But instead, he leaned his head toward hers. "I think it's time for some kisses," he said. Disgusted, Jasmine took a step back as, at the same time, Dalia and Raja stepped forward protectively. The prince retreated and let out a rather high-pitched laugh as he realized he had, perhaps, been a bit too bold in his attempt. "Maybe tomorrow. Why did no one tell me of your beauty?"

"Funny, no one mentioned yours, either," she replied, the dry retort springing from her mouth despite herself. Jasmine couldn't help contrasting the man's ghostly skin, lifeless straw-colored hair, and sense of entitlement against the young man she'd met at the market, with his mop of thick black hair and easygoing charm . . . Remembering her mother's bracelet, she shook her head, refocusing.

"Funny, they say that in Skånland. It's very

amusing," Prince Anders said, trying—and failing—to connect with Jasmine in some way.

Jasmine cocked her head. "Is it?" she retorted, still bristling from his first words to her, the focus on her appearance. "We have the same title, yet are never described the same way." Her words bounced off the walls of the Great Hall as silence descended over the small group. She saw her father shift on his feet, and though she didn't look at him, she could sense Jafar's evil eyes drilling into her with disappointment. She knew what was expected of her. She knew she was supposed to stand there, look pretty, and pretend to be enamored with the attention. But she was so tired of being nothing more than a pawn, a piece to be trotted out when needed and then put back away, silenced in her chambers. She had balanced etiquette lessons with private history lessons. She knew how to pour a proper tea but could also name all the rulers of Agrabah in order of their succession. She had read the works of the greatest philosophers, memorized poetry from around the world, and studied battle warfare—all while keeping up with the day-to-day obligations that went along with being a princess. And yet, no one stopped to ask her what she thought about alliances or new shipping laws. Those questions went to the Sultan and Jafar, while she was left to tackle the deep and weighty questions of what linens they would use or what flowers should be displayed in the front hall. She let out an annoyed sigh.

"Um . . ." Prince Anders stammered, unsure how to proceed. His eyes landed on Raja, standing still beside Jasmine. "What is that? No, don't tell me . . . it's a cat with stripes," he said. Then, puffing out his chest and resuming the role of prince, he smiled smugly. "Cats love me. Hello, kitty—" He leaned forward to pet Raja. The tiger let out a low, deep, and unfriendly snarl.

The prince jumped back with a shrill shriek, spilling a sizable basket of muskmelons. The large beige fruits fell to the floor, some of them splitting open to reveal their orange centers and spattering seeds everywhere. Embarrassed, Prince Anders regained his balance and quickly snapped at one of his attendants. The servant bent down and began to pick up the melons. Jasmine watched, partly amused, partly annoyed.

"I've been told you brought us a special gift from your homeland," the Sultan said, desperate to bring the meeting back under some semblance of control.

The question seemed to do the trick. With a flip of his long cape, Prince Anders led the group over to the balcony. Jasmine's eyes narrowed as she saw the "gift" the prince had brought her father. Another group of attendants were gathered around a huge cannon, its black sides gleaming in the sun.

"In Skånland," Prince Anders said proudly, gesturing at the weapon, "everything we make is, you know, very sleek and, um . . ."

Jasmine wanted to laugh out loud. Was Anders serious? Had he even bothered to look around or see what type of place Agrabah was before he came sailing over the sea on his fancy ship? Agrabah was not a place of weapons or violence. Or at least, it *hadn't* been. "We are a humble people," she said, earning more looks from her father and Jafar, "not impressed with the gift so much as the sentiment behind it."

The princess's words deflated some of Anders's puffed-up ego. "Well, it's . . . it's . . ." he stammered, "a symbol of our . . . our . . ." His voice faded as he struggled for the word.

"Desire for war?" Jasmine finished for him.

"Not . . . no . . ." Prince Anders protested.

Jasmine raised an eyebrow. The man's face was turning a startling shade of red, from embarrassment or anger, it was hard to tell which. She opened her mouth to continue her criticism of the gift when Jafar stepped forward, pushing back the long black cape he wore at all times. Laced with maroon and interspersed with gold accents, the cloak had always seemed, to Jasmine, to be too dark a choice for vibrant Agrabah. But seeing as the man who wore it was one of her least favorite people, she never bothered to offer him fashion advice. The only pop of bright color on Jafar was the turquoise accents on the staff that he never went anywhere without. As she watched now, his long, thin fingers curled around the gold staff adorned with a serpent's head. The vizier's cold eyes fittingly reminded Jasmine of a cobra's right before it attacked a mouse.

"Our princess fails to understand that no man desires war," Jafar said in a smooth and condescending tone. "But a ruler must prepare for it nonetheless."

Jasmine's hands clenched, and beside her, she felt Raja's hackles raise as he sensed his mistress's barely veiled anger. Jafar had no right to talk to her that way. She sighed. Well, he *should* have no right to talk to her that way, but her father wasn't making any move to stop him. Her father wasn't doing much of anything, for that matter. Ignoring the warning look from Jafar that told her to stay quiet, Jasmine continued. "But what if, in preparing, you cause the war you were trying to—"

"Now, now, dear," the Sultan soothed, taking the opportunity to finally speak but offering her no help whatsoever.

"Our princess has read something about statecraft," Jafar said, explaining her thoughts to Prince Anders as though she were a child unable to speak for herself.

Anders nodded. "A charming hobby," he said, equally patronizing.

"The princess is delighted to receive your gift, Prince Anders, as I am," Jafar went on. He smirked, seeming happy to have put Jasmine in her place and aligned himself in the favor of the foreign prince. "Let us see it," he suggested, pointing to the cannon.

Clapping his hands together, Anders nodded. He shouted instructions to his attendants, who began to aim the cannon. "We will target that boat," the prince said, pointing to a lone ship in the middle of Agrabah's harbor. A large target had been painted on its side, and other boats had been moved away to prevent them from being struck by any flying debris. "Prepare yourselves," he announced. With that, he raised his hands and stuck a finger in each ear. An attendant struck a match and lit the fuse. Then they all backed up and waited, fingers in their ears as well.

The flame trickled into the cannon and disappeared, and then . . .

BOOM!

The cannon went off, sending the men flying backward and filling the air with thick smoke. "Very impressive, Prince Anders!" the Sultan said, when the smoke had finally cleared.

"*Ja,*" the prince said, nodding proudly. "It is a very good design."

Looking out to the harbor beyond, Jasmine cocked her head. A smile tugged at the corners of her lips. "Tell me," she said, pointing out at the bright blue water, "which boat were you trying to hit, Prince Anders? Not the one with the target on it?"

Following the direction of her finger, the three

men looked out at the harbor. The target boat, its big painted mark still clearly visible, floated atop the waves, completely unharmed. The cannon had missed its mark. It had not, however, missed *every-thing*. As Prince Anders laughed nervously, they all looked toward a trail of smoke rising up into the air. Following the smoke to its origin, they saw the mast of a ship—or rather, where the mast of a ship *had* been. A flag bearing the symbol of Skånland fluttered from the side that wasn't burning.

"Isn't that one . . . *your* boat?" Jasmine asked, her eyes twinkling.

On Jafar's shoulder, Iago began to repeat, "Your boat, your boat," in his annoying squawking voice. But for once, Jasmine didn't mind.

Aladdin stood hidden among a group of street entertainers. In front of him, merchants, servants, and various dignitaries made their way through one of the palace's main gates. Aladdin's eyes narrowed as he took in the heavily armed guards standing watch. The security made it a sort of fortress.

But he had a plan.

"You know what to do, Abu," Aladdin said, motioning to his furry friend to stay.

The monkey nodded. He had been quite agreeable since showing Aladdin the "borrowed" bracelet. Feeling eyes on him, the tiny monkey looked up, noticing a brightly colored parrot circling above them. He shot the bird a look and chattered angrily. He hated parrots.

Then the monkey scampered over and raced up the leg of one of the guards. As the guard began to shout and swing his arms, Aladdin reached out and grabbed an abandoned cloak off a nearby stall. Flipping the hood over his head, he joined a line of travelers wearing similar garb.

Keeping his head down, Aladdin walked past the guards—and right into the palace.

Chapter
Six

The Sultan's inner sanctum was, despite being the place where the Sultan spent most of his time, a tiny room. Small windows high on the walls allowed some of the late afternoon sun to filter into the room, illuminating the opulent treasures that filled the space. Items collected from all over the world, some given as gifts, others brought home as treasured mementos back when he had traveled with his late wife, lined the shelves and spilled out onto the floor. The Sultan had always loved this part of the palace. Despite its size, it had always felt like a spacious safe haven to him. It was, as the name implied, a sanctuary.

But right then, it felt crowded.

Both Jafar and Hakim stood with their eyes fixed on the Sultan as he absently played with a golden horse. The meeting with Prince Anders had gone horribly. The Sultan knew that. Jasmine had been reckless in her sarcasm, but he couldn't be mad at his daughter. Her spirit was so like that of her mother.

"Our enemies grow stronger every day," Jafar said, his cold voice out of place in the warm room. "Yet you allow your daughter to dismiss Prince Anders and a possible military alliance—"

"Which enemies?" the Sultan interrupted. He was not in the mood to hear Jafar criticize his daughter yet again.

Jafar's fingers tightened around the staff in his hand. "Shirabad continues to amass—"

"Shirabad is our ally," the Sultan corrected. This was a conversation he and his vizier had had already—many, many times. He was growing tired of Jafar's suspicions and accusations. Yet for some reason, he seemed to always end up agreeing with the man in the end. . . . "You would drag us into a war with our oldest—"

This time it was Jafar who interrupted. "And you would allow your kingdom to sink into ruin for mere sentiment."

Anger flashed in the Sultan's eyes. "Jafar!" he snapped. "Remember your place!" The Sultan prided himself on being a calm and peaceful man and ruler. Even as the words left his mouth, he felt guilt for losing his patience with his vizier. But Jafar knew better than to bring up sentiment when it came to Shirabad. Turning, the Sultan looked at his head guard. "You may go, Hakim."

Jafar watched as the man left, shutting the door behind him. When Hakim's footsteps had faded away, Jafar turned back to the Sultan. He was tired of being insulted by this man with his silly heart and inability for action. Yet he had no choice. He was there to serve at the Sultan's command.

Or at least, that is what he allowed the man to believe.

"Forgive me, my sultan," Jafar said. Then, raising his staff, he pointed the metallic snake engraved on the top toward the Sultan. Slowly, the snake's eyes began to glow red. The red grew darker and darker, seeming to pulse with power. Jafar's hand tightened and the power grew. He had kept his powers and connection to magic a secret from the Sultan. It would do him no good if the Sultan realized just how much he "relied" on Jafar. "If you would only reconsider . . ." Jafar said, causing the Sultan to look directly at him—and in turn, the staff. The Sultan's eyes locked on the snake, and instantly, his expression grew dull. He couldn't seem to pull his attention away from the staff.

Jafar smiled sinisterly as he watched the mesmerized Sultan. "I think you'll see that *invading Shirabad is the right thing to do*," he said in a smooth, hypnotic tone.

The Sultan nodded, in a trance. "Invading Shirabad is the right thing—"

"Invade Shirabad?"

Jasmine's voice echoed off the walls of the sanctum, breaking the spell. Jafar stifled a curse as he turned and saw the princess standing in the doorway, suspicion on her face. In a few long strides, she had crossed to her father and taken his hand. She looked at him with a combination of worry and disappointment. "Why would we invade my mother's kingdom?" she asked. "If not for Shirabad, we'd have no access to inland trade—"

"We would never invade Shirabad," the Sultan said, unaware of what he had been about to agree to before his daughter's arrival.

Stepping between father and daughter, Jafar once more lifted his staff, blocking it from Jasmine's view. The snake's eyes grew red as he spoke. "But an ally in Skånland could improve our situation," he said to the Sultan.

Unable to stop himself, the Sultan nodded, once more going along with Jafar's idea. "Yes," he said. "If you would give Prince Anders a chance."

"To rule our people?" Jasmine asked, not bothering to stifle her laugh. "Raja would make a better ruler."

The Sultan did not seem to find her suggestion amusing. His expression grew serious, as did his tone as he spoke. "I'm not getting any younger, my dear. We must find you a husband, and we're running out of kingdoms . . ."

"What foreign prince could care for our people as I do? Why can't I lead—"

"You cannot be sultan," her father said, cutting her off. "Because it has never been done in the thousand-year history of our kingdom."

Jasmine wanted to scream. It wasn't fair. She had read every book there was on her country. She knew the history of Agrabah better than the best scholars, she was sure of it. She had studied the maps and looked at the borders. She knew the alliances and the enemies. And yet none of that mattered—because she hadn't been born a boy.

"I have been preparing for this my whole life," Jasmine tried. "I've read every book."

Jafar's slick voice cut in. "Books!" he said, this time the one to laugh at the idea. "But you cannot *read* experience, Princess."

"Better a leader who cares for her people than—"

Jafar stopped her. "Actually, it isn't," he said, shaking his head. His dark eyes grew darker and his voice dripped with arrogance. "Ignorance is dangerous. People left unchecked will revolt. Walls and borders unguarded will be attacked."

"I'm afraid Jafar is right, my dear," the Sultan said. "The world is a dangerous place."

Nodding, Jafar didn't bother to hide his smile of pleasure at hearing the Sultan's agreement. Emboldened, the vizier stepped forward and put a hand on Jasmine's shoulder. She tried not to visibly shudder at his touch, but her stomach roiled. "We each have an important role to play, Princess. Why not focus on what you do so well and leave these more serious matters to us?"

Jasmine's mouth dropped open and her hands clenched at her sides. Before she could even formulate a response, the two men turned and left, shutting the door behind them. Alone in the sanctum, Jasmine felt a wave of emotion wash over her. What more could she do? What more did she have to say? Every time she had tried to make her father hear her, she had felt as though her voice was drowned out by Jafar's thunderous one. Just thinking his name made the shudder she had held back roll over her. She hated the man. She had heard him described as handsome by some of the servant girls, heard them giggling when he walked by. But she didn't see anything remotely attractive about the man. To her, he was just ugly—inside and out.

Sighing, Jasmine left the room and began walking the halls toward her chambers. Her fingers trailed along the walls. These were the same halls she had been walking down her entire life. The walls were the same ones she had looked at since she was a baby in her mother's arms. Nothing had changed. She was the princess, yet she felt more like a prisoner. Her father didn't want to hear her. He wanted her silent. Jafar wanted her silent *and* married off. No one wanted her to have a voice.

But I'm not going to let them keep me quiet, Jasmine thought as she entered her chambers and walked out onto the balcony. Looking at the city below, *her* city, she nodded. *I'll find a way to prove to them that I'm right. I know I can rule. I just need to make them believe it. . . .*

In his private study, Jafar stared down at the ancient scrolls spread across his desk. Candlelight sent shadows dancing across the weathered vellum, highlighting writing and illustrations and then sending them back into darkness. Most of the writing was faded, barely legible. A few illustrations could be made out in the corners of the pages—a genie's lamp, a carpet that appeared to be flying, the head of a lion.

For years, Jafar had been staring at these same papers. Hidden among them was supposed to be the solution to his predicament—always being *beside* power, but never *holding* it. He would never admit it aloud, but Jasmine wasn't entirely different from him. Well, other than the fact that she wanted to be a ruler to *help* her people, and he wanted to be a ruler to *control* the people. But that aside, they both wanted something that seemed impossible.

Unless . . . unless he could find what he was looking for. . . .

"Remember your place, Jafar?"

Hearing his parrot's voice reciting the Sultan's earlier words, Jafar scowled and looked up. The parrot was perched on his stand by the window, ruffling his feathers. "Another petty insult from that narrow-minded fool," Jafar said, fresh anger filling him. "He sees a city where I see an *empire*." He looked back down at the scrolls. His eyes focused on the faded illustration of a genie's lamp. *That* was his solution. The lamp. If he had read the papers right—and he was sure he had—getting that lamp would solve everything. Getting that lamp and finding a "diamond in the rough." "Once the lamp sits on this desk, I will sit on his throne. I just have to—"

"Thief in the palace!"

Iago's words startled Jafar. He asked the parrot to repeat himself. *A thief in the palace?* Jafar mused as the parrot did what he was told and then resumed his grooming. Walking over to the large window that overlooked the palace courtyard, Jafar scanned the grounds. Iago was his most trusted eyes and ears. He knew the bird was speaking the truth, but all he could see was darkness.

And then, out of the shadows emerged a figure. Squinting, Jafar watched as a young man deftly made his way behind the guards, his feet silent on the ground, his moves those of one who had spent years avoiding trouble. But the young man never resorted to violence, even when, at one point, he almost came face-to-face with a particularly large guard wielding a particularly large sword. A smile began to tug at Jafar's lips as he watched the thief slip through one of the doors off the courtyard. Iago had been right to call his attention to the thief. *I wonder what he's up to,* Jafar thought. *What is he after? It must be good—to risk slipping past so many guards.* He cocked his head. Whoever the thief was, it would be wise for Jafar to keep an eye on him. The young man was clearly skilled in thievery and wily if he could get past the guards. Someone like that could be a problem . . . or a solution. He would have to see which of the two this young man would prove to be.

Chapter
Seven

"There must be something I can do. . . ."

Hearing the desperation in her mistress's voice, Dalia shrugged as she unlaced the back of Jasmine's gown, threading the thick silk through the hundredth eyelet. "A handsome prince wants to marry you," she said, struggling with a particularly hard knot and letting out a squeak as she pinched her finger. "Such a tough life."

Looking up from the map she had been studying, Jasmine turned and playfully stuck her tongue out at her handmaiden. Ever since returning to her chambers, she had been in a funk. Dalia's sarcastic but loving comment at least served to brighten her mood. "You know it's not that I don't want to marry, it's just that . . ." Her voice trailed off. What was the point of saying the words aloud again?

"You want to be sultan," Dalia said for her. "But why would you want to work? I work all the time, and look how tired I am. Doesn't it sound nice to just look out the window . . ." Seeing that her friend was not listening, Dalia's voice trailed off and her sentence went unfinished.

Jasmine didn't notice. Her thoughts were focused on the city beyond the palace walls. Images of her time in the market ran through her mind on a loop. The children starving for attention and food. The new guards with their weapons and quick judgment. Aladdin and his tower home that he had filled with sentimental treasures to make up for missing his lost parents. She shook her head. "My mother always said we could only be as happy as our least happy subject," she finally said, her voice soft and full of emotion. "If she could see what I saw today, she'd be heartbroken. I can help. It's what I was born for, not marrying some useless prince."

Dalia felt a rush of love for her friend. This was not the first time they had had this conversation. Jasmine had loved her mother dearly, and her loss had been devastating. She had lost not just her mother, but a friend, confidante, and ally. The Queen had always encouraged Jasmine to speak her mind and follow her dreams. With her gone,

Jasmine had lost that support. Trying to once again brighten the mood, Dalia smiled playfully. "Well, if you *have* to pick a useless prince, you could do worse than this one." She had seen Prince Anders. "He's tall, handsome in a 'don't speak' kind of way . . ." Jasmine rolled her eyes and Dalia shrugged once more. "Yes, he's an idiot. But you'd prefer that thief from the market?"

Jasmine looked down at her hands, her cheeks flushing red.

"Psst . . ."

Jasmine's head shot up and she locked eyes with Dalia. "What was that?" she asked. Dalia shook her head. Putting a finger to her lips, Dalia leaned through the open door of Jasmine's chamber into the corridor. Seeing no one, she tiptoed out into the hall. Jasmine moved to follow when she suddenly felt a tug on her arm. Before she could even open her mouth to shout for help, she was pulled back into her chambers and the door closed.

Jasmine whipped around, her hands raised in defense, and her eyes grew wide as she came face-to-face with Aladdin. "*You—*" she said, her breath coming out in a whoosh. Her heart was still pounding, but the initial fear was fading, replaced with anger . . . and curiosity. "What are you doing here?" She wasn't sure what she wanted him to say. A part of her wanted him to say he was there to apologize. Another part wanted him to say he'd missed her. A third part—a small, rebellious, and sick-of-her-life-as-it-was part—wanted him to say he had come to take her far away.

Instead, he said, "Returning your bracelet."

Jasmine cocked her head. "My bracelet?" she repeated. Then she looked at his hands, which were empty. "Where is it?"

Smiling, Aladdin nodded toward her arm. "On your wrist," he said.

Sure enough, there it was, wrapped around her wrist as though it had always been there. Jasmine gasped. She lifted her head, and her eyes locked with Aladdin's. She wasn't sure what to say. A thief who *returned* what he had stolen? There was more to Aladdin than she had thought. He wasn't just a thief. He wasn't a prince, either, but he seemed, Jasmine mused, like a good person at heart. Like someone a bit rough around the edges, but with a soft and gentle soul.

As if reading her thoughts, Aladdin shrugged. "See?" he said. "I'm not just a thief." Then, as though the admission embarrassed him, Aladdin's cheeks grew red and he shuffled awkwardly on his feet. He turned and gestured around the chambers. "Not bad, I like what the princess has done with the place."

Jasmine smiled, finding his discomfort oddly cute. As he wandered from the bookshelves to her desk and then over to her window, she could almost forget that the whole reason he was in her chambers in the first place was because he had snuck in—and the fact that he was a thief. "How did you get past the guards?"

"It was challenging, but I have my ways," he said. "While she's out, did you want to go for a stroll and a chat?"

Jasmine's eyes narrowed at his gall. He was incorrigible! He was unbelievable! She stammered and stuttered, trying to find the words to voice her disbelief. "You break in, then walk around like you own the place!" she finally managed to get out.

"When you don't have anything, you have to act like you own everything," Aladdin responded with a shrug. "So, what do you say? I did find your bracelet . . ."

Jasmine had opened her mouth to point out

just how wrong that statement was when, suddenly, there was the sound of rustling fabric and soft footsteps from the hall outside. A moment later, Dalia appeared, her face flushed from trying to track down the mysterious sound.

Seeing the other young woman, Aladdin instantly bowed his head. Jasmine and Dalia exchanged an amused glance. Clearly, Aladdin had presumed Dalia was the princess. *Far be it from me to break him of that illusion,* Jasmine thought, shooting Dalia a look that said, *Just go with it.*

"Your Majesty," Aladdin said, his head still bowed.

Dalia's grin grew wider. "Oh . . . *I'm* the princess. Yes, it's so good to be me . . . to have so many palaces, wagons of gold, things and dresses for every hour of the day. And now, it's time to clean my cat."

Jasmine raised an eyebrow at her friend. Clean her cat? Seriously? That was a bit much. But she couldn't say anything without giving them away, so she shrugged. "She doesn't get out much," she said as Dalia left the room.

"Clearly," Aladdin said, nodding. Then his eyes grew wide.

Turning to see what he was looking at, she smiled. Raja had just walked into the room. Brushing calmly past Aladdin, as though the man's presence in his owner's chambers was a normal occurrence, he flopped down on the ground and began to groom himself.

"Oh, aren't you supposed to be in the bath?" Aladdin said.

From the bathroom, Dalia's voice rang out. "Oh, servant girl, this cat doesn't clean itself." At the sound of her voice, Raja got up and padded in Dalia's direction.

Watching the tiger, Aladdin cocked his head. "Don't cats clean themselves?" he said. "That's sort of their thing."

Before Jasmine could respond, however, more footsteps sounded from the corridor outside. And while Dalia's had been light, these were heavy. Heavy and loud. It had to be Jafar's guards. They must have discovered there was an intruder in the palace. If they found Aladdin in her chambers, he would be thrown in the dungeon, or worse— sentenced to immediate death for fraternizing with the princess of Agrabah. "Time for you to go . . .

now!" Jasmine said, looking frantically around for an exit.

Seeing the panic in her eyes, Aladdin nodded. "Okay, but I'm coming back tomorrow night."

"You can't!" Jasmine exclaimed, shaking her head.

But Aladdin wasn't taking no for an answer. "Tomorrow," he said stubbornly. "Meet me in the courtyard by the fountain when the moon's above the minaret. To return this . . ." Reaching up, he smoothly pulled out a gold hairpin holding Jasmine's thick, dark waves in place. He took one piece and handed her the other. "I promise."

Then he turned and slipped out onto the balcony, disappearing from view.

Jasmine watched him go, a smile tugging at her lips. The guards' footsteps faded and she realized she had just sent Aladdin away for nothing. But he was going to return—tomorrow. And she found the thought of seeing him again more than slightly pleasing.

Still smiling, she turned and headed toward the bathroom. She was going to need Dalia's help if she was going to find a way to keep this whole ruse going. Not to mention she needed to have a little chat with her handmaiden about her "impersonation" skills. . . .

Chapter
Eight

oving down a corridor, Aladdin stared down at the golden hairpin in his hands. His eyes were glazed and a grin spread across his face as he replayed his conversation with Dalia over and over in his head. True, he had snuck in and startled her. And true, he had probably made a fool of himself in front of the princess. And true, he probably could have found a way to see her again *without* taking something that belonged to her. But he hadn't been ready to leave when she'd told him to go, and taking the hairpin meant he had something of hers to hold on to until he saw her again. Which, luckily, was going to be tomorrow. Nothing could stop him—

Except, perhaps, for the large man and guards standing right in front of me, Aladdin thought, coming to a halt. Several heavily armed men glared at him. It turned out he hadn't been as smooth about sneaking into the most heavily guarded place in all of Agrabah as he'd thought. *Probably should have seen this coming,* he thought wryly.

A guard, whom Aladdin took to be the head of the group, stepped forward. He raised his arm over Aladdin's head. Before Aladdin could step out of the way, the guard's hand came down on his head—and the world went black.

Aladdin blinked his eyes open. Immediately, he wished he had kept them shut. The sun blared down at him, bouncing off the sand and nearly blinding him. His head, already pounding from the beating he had taken, began to pulse with pain. Slowly, he sat up and looked around.

He was clearly no longer in the palace . . . nor was he in Agrabah. He was, it seemed, somewhere in the middle of the desert, surrounded by sprawling sand dunes as far as the eye could see, aside from a few trees and a small pool of water, which indicated he had been brought to an oasis. But why? He looked over and saw four camels and two guards standing a few feet away. They were all staring at him, the camels' expressions clearer and brighter than those of the heavily muscled and tiny-brained guards. Nearby, Aladdin heard the familiar sound of Abu's chattering. That, at least, made him feel slightly better.

"Wh-Where am I?" Aladdin asked.

From behind him came a cold, sneering voice. "In a world of trouble, boy."

Turning, Aladdin found himself looking at a tall, thin man with chiseled features. His eyes narrowed. He knew exactly who the voice belonged to. He would recognize the Sultan's evil vizier any day. It was the vizier who had turned the streets of Agrabah into a playground for his team of cruel guards. "I didn't steal that bracelet," Aladdin began, sure that was the reason for his current predicament. "That handmaid, she—"

Jafar cut him off. "What was the handmaid doing wearing the Queen's bracelet?"

"The Queen?" Aladdin repeated, shaking his head. "No . . . she said it belonged to her—"

"Mother?" Jafar finished. At Aladdin's nod, Jafar sneered. "Well, at least she told the truth about one thing. . . ."

Aladdin's head spun. Was Jafar saying what he thought he was saying? Could it even be possible? "That was . . . the *princess*?" It was unimaginable, but Jafar nodded. "I was talking to the princess?" He didn't know whether to be terrified or thrilled.

"She was toying with you," Jafar said icily. "It amuses her to meet commoners."

Aladdin looked down at the half of the hairpin he somehow still clutched in his hand. She had been playacting with him? About everything? He thought back to their moment in his tower, when she had seemed to understand him so well. That couldn't have been an act, could it? His face crumpled. Who was he kidding? Of course it could have been an act. After all, pretending to be something you weren't was how he lived nearly every day of his life. Who was to say a princess couldn't do the same thing?

"Did you think she actually liked you?" Jafar asked, giving Aladdin a pitying smile. He shook his head. "You're hardly the first to be taken in. But make no mistake, she'll marry a prince—and not just because it is decreed." The man looked Aladdin up and down. "What do they call you?"

"Aladdin," he answered.

Jafar nodded, his expression softening. "People like us must be realistic if—"

"*Us?*" Aladdin replied, his eyes narrowing sus- piciously. The comparison seemed unlikely. The vizier was dripping in money and had the air of someone used to the creature comforts of life. It was hard to imagine he had ever had to fight for anything.

But Jafar nodded. "I was once like you . . ." He handed Aladdin the hairpin. Aladdin looked down at the hairpin and then back up at Jafar, shocked. The man had stolen it right out of his hand and Aladdin hadn't even noticed! Jafar went on. "A common thief. Only I thought bigger. Steal an apple and you're a thief. Steal a kingdom and you're a statesman. You're either the most powerful man in the room, or you're nothing." He stopped. Aladdin stared at him, his mind racing as he tried to imagine Jafar on the streets, stealing to sur- vive, struggling for a bite to eat. He couldn't see it. But why would Jafar lie to him? As if reading his thoughts, Jafar went on. "You've stumbled upon an opportunity. I could have your head for what you did . . ."

Aladdin cocked his head. Losing it didn't sound much like an opportunity to him.

"Or I can make you rich," Jafar went on. "Rich enough to impress a princess. But nothing comes for free."

Now *that* sounded more like an opportunity. Aladdin found himself leaning forward, his fingers tightening around the hairpin clutched in his hand. He wasn't a fool. He knew there would be a price before Jafar even said it. He had lived long enough as a street rat to know that every action had a consequence, every coin had two sides. "What would I have to—"

Jafar didn't let him finish. "One small favor is all I ask. There is a cave nearby, and in it, a simple oil lamp. Retrieve it for me and I'll make you wealthy beyond your wildest imagination."

Jafar's words drifted over the oasis. Aladdin knew there was no real choice. If he didn't help the vizier, he would be put to death. He would never see Jasmine again. But if he did help him, he could be rich. Rich and perhaps able to see the princess again. All his life he had been looking for a way to escape his street rat life, to really become someone people would respect. Was this his chance?

"You're nothing to her now . . . but you could

be," the vizier went on, as though reading Aladdin's thoughts. "Your life begins here . . . if you choose it."

Aladdin looked up, his eyes locking on Jafar's. And then, he nodded.

Jasmine stared up at the moon. It hovered over the palace gardens, the bright white light covering the manicured plants and trees and making everything glow. The stars twinkled, and from time to time, birds sang out to one another and frogs croaked from the small ponds, creating a melodic backdrop as Jasmine waited for Aladdin.

But he hadn't arrived yet.

When she had first left her chambers, the moon had just risen over the horizon. But now it was almost directly above her, and still no Aladdin. Hearing footsteps behind her, Jasmine turned excitedly. But the smile faded when she saw it was only Dalia.

"Still waiting for the boy who's a thief with the monkey on his shoulder?" the handmaiden asked.

"No, no. I, uh, just came out to . . ." Her voice

trailed off. She wasn't fooling anyone. She let out a sigh and her shoulders slumped. "He promised," she said softly. She was surprised to hear the disappointment in her voice. She had seen Aladdin a grand total of two times. They had had one moment in the tower. And yet, there was just something about him. She felt a connection to him, a rare soul who had seemed to understand exactly what she was going through, who respected what she had to say. But if he didn't show up, how would she ever get to find out what that meant? And where that could lead?

"Men make promises, it's what they do. They also whistle and spit, like the butcher's son Rashid, whose dog took to my ankle in such a violent way. Scars on my ankle, scars on my heart." Dalia put a hand on Jasmine's shoulder and gave it a gentle squeeze. "I'll be upstairs if you need me. . . ."

Jasmine nodded, returning her gaze to the moon. She knew she should go upstairs, too. But not quite yet. She would wait just a little longer. Maybe he was making his way toward the palace now. Maybe he was looking up at the moon, too, trying to get to her. . . .

Chapter
Nine

I blew it, Aladdin thought as he followed Jafar across the desert. The moon was sinking quickly, and he knew that back at the palace, Jasmine was probably—well, hopefully—waiting for him in the garden. But he wasn't going to show up. And he couldn't tell her that the reason he wasn't there was because he was following the Sultan's vizier through the desert to help him find a lamp that was somehow going to help the vizier take over the world and make Aladdin rich. Because, if he was honest with himself, that sounded pretty far-fetched.

On his shoulder, Abu was chattering away. Aladdin nodded at his friend and opened his mouth to say something reassuring when, suddenly, Jafar pulled his camel to a stop. The animal grunted, and Aladdin quickly pulled back on his own reins, startling Abu and causing the camel they rode to let out its own protest.

Jafar was staring intently at a particular dune of sand. Aladdin narrowed his eyes and followed the vizier's gaze, trying to see what was so interesting. There was nothing to distinguish it from the rest of the dunes around them. But then, as Aladdin watched, the sand began to shift and move. It undulated, like waves across the ocean. Aladdin took a nervous step back as a deep rumbling filled the air and the ground beneath his feet began to shake. The camels pulled violently at their reins, the unnatural noises and movements spooking them. Suddenly, there was a loud rumble, and emerging from under the desert itself, a giant lion's head appeared, its mouth open in mid-roar. Abu let out a screech and wrapped his tail around Aladdin's neck.

"The Cave of Wonders," Jafar said, a triumphant smile on his face. "No one's been worthy to enter in many years." He turned and looked at Aladdin. "But I see you are the one to succeed where others have failed."

"Me?" Aladdin repeated. What was so special about him? He was still just a common street rat. But Jafar was nodding. Maybe he wasn't so common after all.

Jafar went on. "When you enter the cave, you see more riches than you've ever dreamed of— gold, silver, diamonds . . . and the lamp. Bring it to me and I will make you rich and free. But take no other treasure, no matter how sorely you are tempted. . . ." He paused, staring intently at Aladdin. "And you *will* be tempted."

Nodding, Aladdin began to walk toward the entrance of the cave. *Nothing but the lamp. Ignore the heaps of gold and diamonds and just take the lamp. Got it,* he thought, pausing in front of the huge gaping lion. After all, how much treasure could be hidden in the mouth of a magical sand lion in the middle of the desert?

Aladdin took a deep breath and started to enter the cave. But as he walked into the lion's mouth, a gust of wind blew up from the depths of the cave. With it came a whispered warning: *Only one may enter here,* Aladdin heard on the wind. *One whose worth lies far within, a "diamond in the rough."* Above, the lion's eyes began to glow.

Letting out another squawk of fear, Abu tightened his grip on Aladdin. Before Aladdin could offer any words of comfort, the sand beneath his feet began to fall away, pulling him and Abu farther into the cave. Aladdin's arms windmilled in the air as he struggled to keep his balance on the shifting sand. It was as though the sand was pulling them forward, toward something. When it finally stopped moving, Aladdin found himself looking down a long, steep flight of staggered steps. They appeared to descend deep into the heart of the cave, the distance between the steps growing wider as they went on.

Aladdin sighed. It looked like he and Abu had no choice. They were venturing farther. *Just like jumping from rooftop to rooftop in Agrabah,* he thought. *With a much bigger prize than a few stolen apples waiting for me at the other end.* His silent pep talk over, Aladdin began to jump down the steps, picking up speed as the distance between them grew longer and the pitch steeper. Over and over again he leapt, each step bringing him farther from the exit but closer to what was hopefully unimaginable treasure. Finally, with one last huge leap, he landed on the floor of the cave.

Instantly, the fear and uncertainty he had been feeling disappeared.

For in front of him, reaching from the floor of the cave high into the air, was treasure. Mounds of treasure. More treasure than Aladdin had thought possible. The room sparkled and gleamed and twinkled and shone. There were piles of diamonds that reached Aladdin's waist. Statues of pure gold were strewn throughout the cave. He saw horses and camels and challises and plates. And the gems! There were hundreds of thousands of sapphires and rubies and emeralds, enough to fill every room of the palace and every vendor's stall in the market of Agrabah.

Beside him, Abu was uncharacteristically quiet. The monkey's little eyes were nearly popping out of his head as he looked around at all the treasure. Slowly, he reached out his little hand to touch a huge sapphire that shimmered next to him. Instantly, the cave rumbled.

"Abu!" Aladdin chastised. Jafar—and the cave itself—had warned them. They weren't supposed to grab anything except the lamp. "Don't touch anything," he said, placing Abu back on his shoulder.

Slowly and carefully, Aladdin began to make his way through the cave. His eyes drifted over more and more riches, the jewels appearing to grow larger as they went. Jafar hadn't been kidding when he'd said there was more treasure down there than one could imagine. Aladdin had spent a *lot* of time imagining treasure. But even he had never thought there could be this much in one place. It was a thief's version of paradise. Or not, because he couldn't touch anything.

Suddenly, out of the corner of his eye, Aladdin saw a gem bigger than any he had seen yet. It was fixed to the wall, just an arm's length away. It gleamed brilliantly, as if asking to be plucked from its spot. Aladdin's hand began to tremble, and before he could stop himself, his fingers stretched toward the jewel. His fingertips itched, the longing to touch the jewel blurring Aladdin's mind and making him forget Jafar's warning.

Just as he was about to grab the gem, Aladdin shook his head, breaking the trance and falling backward. He let out a cry as he fell. With a muffled thud, he landed on something soft. Turning, he saw that he had fallen onto a purple carpet. Sliding off and getting back to his feet, he cocked his head. The rug appeared to be floating about a foot off the ground. Aladdin leaned down, trying to see how it was suspended. Was it caught on something? Maybe there was a candlestick or something underneath that he couldn't see. But no matter where Aladdin looked, he could find nothing to explain how the carpet was floating. He shook his head. There was no way this was possible. Unless . . . His mouth dropped open and his eyes grew wide as he finally realized exactly what type of rug he was looking at. He had *heard* stories, but he had thought they were just that—stories. Apparently not. "Abu, is this a *magic* carpet?" To his surprise, it was the carpet, not Abu, who answered. The rug began to nod. "Well, hello, Carpet," Aladdin marveled.

Pleased, the carpet waved its tassels. Pleasantries done, the carpet swished left and then right and then stopped, pointing one of its tassels straight at a large chest. Following the tassel, Aladdin saw that a corner of the carpet was caught under the chest. "Oh! Let's see what we can do about your situation here." Aladdin pushed the chest aside, and the carpet sprung loose and began to fly around Aladdin and Abu.

Thrilled to be free, the carpet spread its tassels for a hug. This did not please Abu, who began chattering angrily and then went to attack the flying floor-covering. "Easy, Abu," Aladdin said, trying to calm his friend down. "He's just saying hello." Then Aladdin's expression grew thoughtful. The carpet was clearly happy to see them. Which meant it had been down there for a long time. Which meant . . . maybe it could *help* them. "We're looking for a brass lamp—"

Aladdin didn't even need to finish his question. The carpet pointed one of its tassels toward the heart of the cave. Large rocky pillars formed a circle and rose into the air, their tops ending long before the ceiling. In the center of the circle, surrounded by small uneven pillars that rose like stairs, sat a brass lamp. In the semidarkness of the cave, it seemed to glow, making the surrounding area brighter. Aladdin nodded. *Well, that wasn't too hard,* he thought. Walking along a small path passing through the treasure, Aladdin approached the outcropping that held the lamp. Abu and the carpet followed close behind.

Reaching the pillars, Aladdin turned to the carpet. "Can you do me a favor? Will you look after my monkey? I'll be back before you know it." The carpet nodded. Then Aladdin looked at Abu. "Keep your monkey hands to yourself," he warned. Turning, he began to make his way up the pillars. Behind him, he could hear Abu's angry squawks.

Aladdin knew the monkey was mad at him for making him stay behind, but he had no choice. There was too much at risk. And the treasure *was* tempting — even for him. And he wasn't a monkey with sticky fingers.

While it hadn't looked that difficult to reach from far away, the lamp was higher up than Aladdin had first thought. And getting to it meant leaping from one rocky, uneven pillar to the next. The leaping part wasn't hard for Aladdin. But avoiding grabbing or touching the random gems that covered the tops of the pillars was proving difficult. Several times, Aladdin's hand accidentally brushed over a large piece of jewelry or a solid piece of gold. And in each instance, the cave rumbled a warning. As he leapt to the final pillar that held the lamp, he accidentally knocked into the largest diamond he had ever seen. Nervously, he watched as it fell, then let out a sigh of relief when the cave didn't protest. He turned his attention to the lamp.

On the ground below, Abu was not so quick to ignore the gem. He had promised Aladdin he wouldn't touch anything. But that was growing increasingly difficult as his pal continued to send jewels rolling down toward him. The carpet had managed to pull Abu back for the most part. But then the giant diamond rolled to a stop—right in front of the monkey. It glittered and gleamed, its facets mesmerizing. Slowly, Abu reached out. His hand came closer and closer . . .

Up above, Aladdin's fingers inched toward the gleaming lamp. In one quick move, he snatched it up. "Ha-ha!" he cried. As he looked down to show Abu, Aladdin's eyes grew wide and he let out a frightened shout.

But it was too late. Abu's little hand had closed around the diamond.

Instantly, the cave let out a monstrous growl. The whole room began to rumble and shake, splitting one of the cave walls wide open. A river of molten lava began to pour out, melting gold and jewels instantly. A moment later it barreled into the pillar that Aladdin was clinging to, knocking it over. A scream caught in his throat as Aladdin was sent flying down—straight toward the deadly lava.

Just in time, the carpet swooped up and caught him. Landing on the carpet's surface, Aladdin let out a triumphant shout as they began to swerve around falling pillars and waves of lava, heading toward the exit. Aladdin's shout died on his lips as he realized Abu was not on the carpet with him. Scanning the quickly flooding cave for his friend, he finally spotted him clinging to a rock. Lava licked at the top of it, making the monkey jump up and down. Aladdin steered the carpet toward Abu. When they were close enough, the monkey leapt up and into Aladdin's arms.

The cave let out another angry rumble.

Aladdin didn't get it. He had just taken the lamp. Nothing else. And Abu had dropped the gem. So why was the cave still so angry? Unless . . . His eyes narrowed and he frowned at his friend. "Abu?" he said, his voice loaded with the unanswered question. The monkey shrugged. "Abu!" Aladdin repeated. This time Abu grinned sheepishly, revealing a mouthful of gems.

As Abu finally spit out the jewels, the carpet continued to fly toward the cave's entrance. But the tremors were growing stronger, and now rocks were beginning to fall from the ceiling, the cave collapsing around them. As the rocks hit the lava, they sent up huge sprays of hot liquid. Swooping left and right, up and down, the carpet managed to avoid being hit or burnt, but the entrance was still far away, and the cave was filling up fast. Urging his new friend on, Aladdin clutched the front of the carpet and held his breath.

The stairs, which had been long and treacherous when they'd first arrived, suddenly appeared as a short stack in front of them. Lava lapped at the top of what was left of them. The cave entrance, which had been huge, was now a tiny hole of an opening. Squinting, Aladdin spotted Jafar standing near the entrance, a torch in his hand, like a beacon of light illuminating the way home.

We made it! Aladdin thought. *Wait till I tell Jasmine about this!*

But just then, a huge rock fell from the ceiling, hitting the carpet. Aladdin and Abu were sent flying. Flailing their arms, they flew through the air, landing with a painful thud on a ledge just below the cave's entrance. Aladdin gripped the lamp while trying to keep him and Abu on the ledge. Spotting them, Jafar ran over.

"Can you give me a hand?" Aladdin shouted.

"First the lamp!" Jafar shouted back.

Aladdin shook his head. "*First*, your hand!"

"You must trust me, Aladdin," Jafar said. "Give me the lamp."

Underneath him, the ledge was giving way. Slowly at first, the rock began to fall into the lava, then faster and faster. Abu clung to Aladdin's neck, making it hard for him to breathe. The lamp hung from his belt, bouncing off his swinging legs. He wasn't going to be able to hang on for much longer. There was no choice left. And, after all, the lamp was why he was in this predicament in the first place. He had promised to give it to Jafar. So what did it matter if he gave it to him now? If he waited, he might fall to his death. Lifting the lamp, he offered it up to Jafar. "Now, your hand!"

"How about my foot?" Jafar answered. With lightning-quick speed, Jafar snatched the lamp and slipped it into the satchel he had over his shoulder. Then he slammed his foot down on Aladdin's hand. As Aladdin screamed in pain, Jafar turned and began to head back out of the cave, leaving Aladdin dangling off the ledge.

If he could have, Aladdin would have hit himself. How had he not seen that coming? Jafar had admitted he was a con artist before he had been a vizier. Of *course* he would have played him for the fool! And now Jafar was walking away with his precious lamp, while Aladdin was probably going to fall to a fiery death.

But Abu was not about to let Jafar get away with it. Chittering angrily, he pushed off of Aladdin's head and leapt onto solid ground. As the cave continued to rumble, Abu leapt onto Jafar's shoulders and began to bat at his face. Jafar shouted and waved his arms, trying to dislodge the creature, but Abu hung on tight.

Just then, the cave gave one last terrible roar, and a huge tremor sent Aladdin flying backward. At the same moment, Abu was sent tumbling off Jafar's shoulders and back toward the ledge. Jafar, free of his tormentor, raced out of the cave just as the huge face of the lion closed and was swallowed up in a billow of dust.

When the shaking and rumbling stopped, the Cave of Wonders was gone—and so, too, it seemed, were Aladdin and Abu.

Chapter

Ten

Aladdin didn't want to open his eyes. Things had grown quiet. Still. He felt oddly at peace. He was resting on something quite soft, and it almost felt like he was floating.

Floating!

Aladdin's eyes popped open. Sitting up, he realized he *was* floating. Sort of. He was on the back of the carpet, which was drifting just a few inches above the ground of the cave. But more importantly—they were alive! The magical carpet must have snatched them out of the air just before Aladdin and Abu both plummeted to their deaths. "We're alive, I think. Thank you, Carpet!" Aladdin cried, hugging the big rug.

The carpet wiggled its tassels happily, and Aladdin began to look around. His smile turned into a frown. Black dust and ash covered nearly every surface, muting what was left of the jewels.

A huge portion of the ceiling had collapsed and the stairs had vanished, covered in lava that was now cooling and hardening. Melted gold and jewels formed glittering towers. But there did not seem to be an exit.

They were trapped.

Hearing an odd sound, Aladdin turned to see Abu diving in and out of the rubble and jewels like a dolphin playing in the waves. Aladdin's eyes narrowed and he cocked his head. "I don't think we can go that way—" he started to say. But the words died on his lips as he saw what was sitting on the ground next to Abu. *The lamp.* Aladdin let out a triumphant shout. "We got it, cunning little monkey!" He could only imagine how angry Jafar was going to be when he realized he had lost his precious artifact. Rejuvenated, Aladdin looked at his friends. "Now all we need's a way out."

Unfortunately, getting into the cave—as hard as that had been—was the easy part. No matter where Aladdin looked, he couldn't figure out a plan of escape.

"Hey, Carpet, do you know if there's a way out of here?" Aladdin asked.

In answer, the carpet shook his tassels in an obvious no.

Letting out a sigh, Aladdin reached down and picked up the cause of their current predicament. He held the lamp in his hands, examining its worn sides, its original color faded and dull. He didn't get it. Why had Jafar been so intent on getting *this*? They had nicer lamps back in the market in Agrabah. Not to mention its value seemed miniscule in comparison to the jewels that littered the cave. He pulled at the lid. Maybe there was something inside? But the lid wouldn't budge. He raised it closer to his eyes and looked down the long spout. He couldn't see anything that way. Just as he was about to put it down, he noticed there was something written on the lamp's side. "What's it say?" he asked aloud. Tugging at his shirtsleeve, he began to rub at the dirt that obscured the writing. More of the text appeared, but it was still unreadable. Aladdin paused. Maybe there was a reason the writing was hard to make out . . . Maybe he should just put it down and walk away. Then he shook his head, brushing the thought aside, and rubbed harder.

Suddenly, a trail of blue smoke began to emerge from the spout. It billowed faster and faster, filling the cave and causing Aladdin to leap back in fright. Abu raced up his shoulder, chittering in alarm. Aladdin's mouth dropped open as a roar echoed out of the smoke, its sound bouncing off the walls and nearly knocking him off his feet. Frantically, he looked around for something to defend himself with, a way to protect himself from whomever—or whatever—was concealed by that smoke. But the ground around him was bare. Taking a deep breath, Aladdin waited to see what would emerge.

When the smoke cleared, there, standing nearly fifty feet tall, was a huge blue man with a swirl of smoke for legs. Two gold cuffs—one on each enormous wrist—glittered in the dim light of the cave as the creature raised his arms into the air and . . . stretched, as though waking from a long nap.

"Oh, Great One who summons me and Terrible One who commands me," the massive blue man said in a dry voice, "I stand by my oath. Loyalty to wishes three . . ." The man's voice faded as he looked down and saw Aladdin and Abu. The pair were staring up at him with wide eyes, their mouths gaping. The being cleared his throat. "I *said*, 'Oh, Great One who summons me and Terrible'—" He stopped again when his clearly well-practiced spiel was still not producing a reaction. He sighed. "Kid, where's your boss?"

As he stared up at the giant who had appeared from the lamp, Aladdin's mind raced. What was going on? How had that happened? Was this another trick of the cave? A thousand questions flooded through him, but for some reason, he couldn't speak. He was rooted to the spot, his eyes glued to the newcomer.

"If I was going to talk to myself I would have stayed in the lamp," the big blue man said. "Just so you know, your mouth is wide open. There's spit coming out, just no words."

"I'm . . . I'm . . ." Aladdin sputtered.

"Use your big-boy voice," the blue man prompted.

Aladdin shook his head. The big guy had a point. He couldn't just keep standing there like a statue. But he couldn't wrap his mind around what was happening. "I am talking to a smoking blue giant who just—"

The blue man raised a finger, stopping Aladdin. The finger, being nearly double Aladdin's entire length, made him take a step back nervously. "We are getting off on the wrong foot here. I am not a giant, I am a *genie*," he corrected. "Big difference. Giants are not real." Seeing that his words seemed to have no effect on Aladdin, the Genie let out another big sigh. "What's your name?" he asked again. Softly, Aladdin spoke his name. The Genie shrugged. "That's weird. Where's your boss?"

"My boss?" Aladdin repeated, confused.

The Genie shot him a look that, if he hadn't already felt minuscule, would have made him feel tiny. "I've been doing this a long time," the Genie explained. "There's always a guy. You know . . . a guy . . . with that *look* in his eye. That chin, eyebrows, tight face. He's always cheated someone, buried someone, or . . . you get my point." He looked Aladdin up and down. "You don't fit the profile. Where's *that* guy?"

As the Genie spoke, Aladdin nodded, a picture of Jafar forming in his mind. "He's outside," Aladdin answered.

The Genie raised one exceptionally large eyebrow. The gold hoops through his ears wiggled as he leaned a bit closer to Aladdin. "So . . . it's just you and me in here?" he asked. Abu let out an annoyed screech, unhappy to be ignored. The carpet shrugged. "And a monkey. We'll talk about that later." He paused, seeming to really see Aladdin for the first time. His eyes wandered over the young man's dirty rags and bare feet, returning finally to his face, the eyes wiser than the years would suggest. "So *you* rubbed the lamp?" Aladdin nodded. "Okay. I've been cramped up in there for a minute, if I could just stretch it out over here, do you mind?"

"Why are you asking me?" Aladdin asked.

The Genie looked genuinely surprised by Aladdin's question. "Um . . . cuz you're my master?" he said. He sighed and sat down with a thud on top of one of the pillars. It looked like he was going to have to do a lot of spelling things out for this kid. Usually the guys who rubbed the lamp knew exactly what they were doing and what they were going to get out of it. But looking down at Aladdin, he could tell the boy was truly not . . . getting . . . it.

First, though, he needed to stretch. He raised his arms high over his head and then bent down toward the ground, the cave echoing with the sound of bones long stuffed in confinement cracking and bending and loosening. Listening to the rather unpleasant sounds, including the long, low moan the Genie let out after a particularly bendy stretch, Aladdin winced. "How long have you been trapped in there?"

In response, the Genie raised his hands, and out of thin air an abacus appeared, its round brightly colored balls sliding back and forth as it magically counted. Then a sundial materialized, followed by a calendar, its pages flipping furiously. " 'Bout a thousand years," the Genie finally answered.

"A thousand years?" Aladdin repeated, his jaw dropping. Somehow this seemed more shocking than the bursts of magic he had just witnessed.

"Kid, is it me or are you surprised at everything?" the Genie asked, reading Aladdin's look. When Aladdin didn't answer, the Genie grew thoughtful. His expression deepened, his thick black eyebrows furrowed. Was it possible that this kid really didn't know who—or rather, *what*—he was? It seemed hard to believe, but . . . "Seriously?"

he pressed. "Genie. Wishes. None of that ringing a bell?" Aladdin shook his head. Next to him, the monkey did the same.

Genie shook his head. He was going to have to do something about this. Lifting a finger into the air, he gestured for Aladdin, Abu, and the carpet to hold a beat.

But they didn't have to wait long. As Genie began to move around the cave, treasure began to come to life. Small things at first—a ring tapping on a tray, two bejeweled plates coming together like tambourines, gold coins righting themselves and rolling down a pile of treasure like a golden stream. Looking to see if Aladdin was impressed, the Genie frowned. Not quite. But how could he *not* be impressed? There was no way that Aladdin had ever had a friend even remotely as amazing, powerful, or downright incredible as the Genie. The Genie was the stuff of legends. Like Ali Baba with his forty thieves, or Scheherazade with her tales that kept her safe for a thousand nights, those who had Genie as a friend had one pretty powerful ally.

With another magical swish of his fingers, the Genie threw Aladdin onto the back of a camel being washed by a dozen identical genies. Aladdin's rags disappeared, replaced by the luxurious garb of a shah. The Genie's hand continued to wave, and one after another, magical illusions appeared— each image grander and more amazing than the last. With one last huge wave of his hand, the air exploded in colorful fireworks that illuminated the dark cave and then fell to the ground in a ripple of gold and silver.

"Uhh, you can clap now," the Genie said, his performance over.

Instantly, Aladdin and the others began to clap. Even the carpet got into it, shaking his tassel tail with excitement. None of them had ever seen anything like that. Ever.

"Thank you, thank you," the Genie said, taking a bow. "You can thank me outside in the sunshine . . . when you wish us out."

Aladdin frowned. "So, how does it work?"

"What?" the Genie cried incredulously. Had the kid not just seen his song and dance? He had explained everything. He let out a big sigh. "Try to pay attention," he said. "Sorry, tell me your name one more time."

"Aladdin," Aladdin offered up once again.

"Yes, yes, Aladdin, Aladdin," the Genie said. "Rhymes with . . ." He stopped and put a finger to his lips. "That's the problem right there. It's your fault, not mine. So, here's the basics. Step one: rub the lamp. Step two: say what you want. Step three . . ." He paused, then smiled impishly. "There is no step three. See, it's *that* easy. You have three wishes and they must begin with rubbing the lamp and saying, 'I wish,' got it?"

Aladdin nodded. "Think so."

There *were* a few rules. Quickly, the Genie ran through them as Aladdin listened, trying to wrap his head around what was happening. He had been trying to play it cool, but as the Genie kept magically creating illusions and talking about wishes—and how they could go terribly wrong— Aladdin began to feel slightly overwhelmed. The rules, it appeared, were put in place to *keep* things from going terribly wrong. For example, he couldn't wish to bring someone back from the dead, or see into the past, or look into the future. "Normally, I don't have to go through this because by the time 'the guy' gets to me he usually knows what he wants," the Genie went on. Aladdin thought of Jafar. He was pretty sure he knew what the vizier

was after. As if reading his mind, the Genie clari-
fied. "Generally has to do with acres of money and
power. Do me a favor, do not drink from that cup. I
promise you there is not enough money and power
on earth for you to be satisfied . . . got it?"

His rules and regulations finished, the Genie
let out a huge sigh. As if he were a balloon deflat-
ing, he began to shrink until, finally, he was about
the same height as Aladdin. He was still way more
muscular, though. And way more blue.

"Okay, well . . . the first thing, we gotta get out
of this cave," Aladdin said.

"No, let's stay. It's so cold and dank and dark
and dungeon-like . . ." Genie said, his voice dripping with sarcasm. "I'm kidding! It's time to go.
Come on, kid, wish us out of here!" He clapped his
hands together, then wrung them nervously.

The movement was not lost on Aladdin. Nor
was the fact that the Genie had been locked away
for a thousand years. He wanted out of that cave
more than anything—probably more than Aladdin
wanted to make a wish. The street rat in Aladdin
perked up.

"I have to think about it, I mean if there are
only three . . ." he said, making a show of looking

thoughtful, as though he were pondering a major life choice. "Why *are* there only three, anyway?" He held up the lamp and moved it up and down. He shrugged, unimpressed.

"I don't know," the Genie said, flustered by getting a question rather than a wish. He shrugged. "Who cares?"

"Where does this cosmic power even come from?" Aladdin pressed.

The Genie groaned in frustration. "Cosmic power? Why are you asking about cosmic power? Let's take this outside in the sun."

"I just want to know how it works," Aladdin said with a shrug.

"I don't know!" the Genie shouted, all his patience gone.

Aladdin bit back a smile. The Genie was playing into this perfectly. "You don't know?" he said, putting a hand to his heart as though shocked. "I thought you were all-knowing."

The Genie shook his head. "I never said I was all-knowing," he corrected. "I said *all-powerful*. Why are you playing hard to wish?"

"So what happens when you encounter another

genie?" Aladdin continued, goading the magical being on. "If you're the most powerful—"

"If I'm out and a genie squares off on me, because genie recognizes genie . . ." The Genie stopped and shook his head. He was done with the conversation. It was time to get a move on. "You are making my heart hurt right now. Look, I know you can't tell this, but I am very pale right now." He held out a blue arm and waved it in front of Aladdin's face. "This is sky blue, but my natural pigmentation is navy. We need some sun."

Distracted by his own lighter-than-desired shade of blue, the Genie didn't notice as Aladdin deftly slipped the lamp out of his hands and into the outstretched hand of Abu. With the lamp safely out of his hands, he nodded. "Genie," he said, "I wish you to get us out of this cave."

"Yes! Boom!" the Genie cried, clapping his hands together excitedly. "He has made his first wish. Never let that lamp out of your sight. No lamp, no wishes." He looked around. Spotting the carpet and Abu, he gestured them over. Abu hopped on the back of the carpet and a moment later, so did Aladdin. As the Genie began to wave his hands in the air, he let out a laugh. "Thanks for choosing carpets, camels, and caravans. Don't forget to tip your genie!"

Slowly they lifted into the air, the Genie beside them. In moments, they were zooming straight up—right toward what looked like solid rock! But to Aladdin's surprise, when the Genie hit the rock, he just disappeared *into* it. A moment later, a hole burst open, big enough to allow the carpet—and his passengers—through. Ahead of them, the Genie tore into the rock, ripping and rending through it until, finally, the last of the rock shattered and they burst into the wide-open and sunlit sky.

The Genie had done it! They were free!

Chapter
Eleven

"**M**an! Look at this world!"

Aladdin, who had had the misfortune to be flung quite unceremoniously off the carpet after exiting the cave, stood up, brushing the sand off his pants. Beside him, Abu did the same. Then they both turned to look at the Genie, who was swimming in the air, performing flips and dives like a caged bird who had been set free.

"It's so . . . big!" Genie cried. "Inside the lamp, everything is like brass, brass—oh, look, more brass." He paused, as if trying to think of anything else that might be in the lamp. Coming up blank, he shrugged and floated down to stand beside Aladdin. "That's the problem with genie life: phenomenal cosmic powers—itty-bitty living space."

Picking up the lamp, which had safely made it out of the cave with Abu, Aladdin held it up to the sun. "So is this magic," he asked, "or are *you* magic?"

"Kind of a package deal," the Genie answered. He snapped his fingers, and a tent appeared over them as Aladdin felt himself plopped into a chair.

"Can you warn me next time?" Aladdin said, although he had to admit being out of the direct desert sun was a relief. He hadn't loved the cold cave but he didn't much like boiling, either. "So, do I have to make all my wishes here?" he asked, gesturing around at the empty desert. "I mean, if I take you back to Agrabah, won't people . . ."

The Genie didn't let him finish. "No, no, no," he said. "I can look totally normal." As if to prove his point, he poofed once more, transforming himself into a human wearing an elaborate, over-the-top blue outfit. On his head he wore a giant hat.

But he was still blue. And still huge.

Aladdin raised an eyebrow. "Totally normal."

Looking down at his large blue hand, the Genie waved it in the air again. This time, when the magical smoke disappeared, the Genie had transformed into a regular-sized human with a smaller hat.

Still blue.

The Genie waved his hand one more time.

As the smoke dissipated, the Genie, now looking like a normal human wearing a normal-sized hat, nodded with satisfaction. "So . . . what are you going to wish for?"

Aladdin shrugged. "I haven't really thought about it," he said. That wasn't *entirely* true. He had definitely spent some nights lying in his tower, wishing things were different. And there had been plenty of days spent scrounging for food when he had wondered *What if . . . ?* But he had honestly never really thought that wishing would get him anywhere. . . .

The Genie shook his head at Aladdin's response. "You are definitely *not* 'that guy,'" he said. But while his tone was disapproving, Aladdin couldn't help noticing that a spark of respect flashed in the Genie's eyes.

"What would *you* wish for?" he asked.

The Genie looked surprised. "Wow," he said after a pause. "Nobody's ever asked me that before.

But that's easy. To be free. To be my own master. Be human."

"Why don't you just set yourself free?" Aladdin asked, confused. Wasn't that a perk of being all-powerful? Couldn't you do whatever you wanted?

The Genie laughed loudly, the sound bouncing off the sand dunes and echoing back at them. Finally, composing himself, he elbowed the rug next to him. "Carpet, did you hear that?" The carpet nodded, clearly in on the joke that Aladdin wasn't getting. Looking back at Aladdin, the Genie explained. "The only way a genie gets free is if the owner of the lamp uses one of his wishes to set him free, and that happens like never—"

"I'll do it," Aladdin said, cutting him off. "I've got three, right?"

"Two—" the Genie corrected. "You already used one."

Aladdin raised an eyebrow, a mischievous smile tugging at his lips. "Did I?" he said. "Or did you? Thought *I* had to rub the lamp."

The Genie narrowed his eyes. Then he threw a hand in the air. The world around them appeared to pause. An image of what had happened in the cave materialized, and Aladdin saw all of them—the Genie, himself, Abu, the carpet—all together. It was the moment right before they'd escaped from the cave. As he watched, the scene began to move in reverse and showed him slyly giving Abu the lamp. A moment later, the Genie turned to smoke and they escaped.

When the scene ended, the image disappeared with a puff of smoke. "Wow," the Genie said. "Street guy, huh? I'm going to have to keep my eye on you . . ." He nodded, looking impressed.

Aladdin shrugged. "At least I can use my third wish to set you free."

The Genie raised his head, his eyes, now a human shade of brown, looking into Aladdin's with a mixture of hope and worry. Then the little bit of hope vanished and he sighed. "Funny thing about wishes," he said, his voice resonating with a thousand years' worth of experience, "the more you get, the more you want. Gotta watch out for that. I've seen it drive people mad."

Aladdin shook his head. "That's not me." Then he paused, unsure if he should go on. But the Genie *had* said he could have any wish he wanted. What good would it be to waste that kind of gift? Especially . . . His eyes clouded over as he thought about the one thing that would make him truly happy.

Seeing the expression, the Genie smiled. He knew that look. "Who's the girl?" he asked. Flying over, the carpet swooped under Genie, who lay down and put his head on his hands. Then he gazed up at Aladdin, looking much like a young person waiting to hear the latest gossip.

Aladdin's cheeks reddened. "She's a princess—"

"They all are." The Genie nodded. "Treat your lady like a queen, I say."

"No, she's an *actual* princess," Aladdin corrected.

Taking his head off his hands, the Genie sat up. "Told you I can't make anyone love anyone, so if she's not feeling you, there's nothing I can do."

"We had a connection," Aladdin argued.

Genie looked over at Abu. "Did they?" he asked.

Abu frowned but nodded reluctantly.

Ignoring the monkey, Aladdin continued. "She's smart, kind, beautiful . . . but she has to marry a

Aladdin is very resilient and agile.

Princess Jasmine visits the marketplace in disguise.

Aladdin leads Princess Jasmine through the marketplace.

Jafar, an evil Sorcerer, uses his staff to control the Sultan.

Aladdin sneaks into the palace to see Princess Jasmine.

Jafar makes a deal with Aladdin.

Aladdin sees many treasures inside the Cave of Wonders.

Aladdin disguises himself as Prince Ali and arrives on a large float to impress Princess Jasmine.

Genie gives Aladdin advice on how to impress Princess Jasmine.

Princess Jasmine asks Aladdin to show her Ababwa, Prince Ali's kingdom, on one of her maps.

Jafar finds the magic lamp.

Jafar takes control of Agrabah.

Princess Jasmine agrees to marry Jafar to protect her father.

Aladdin and Princess Jasmine team up to overthrow Jafar.

prince . . ." His voice trailed off and his eyes brightened. "Hey! Can you make me a prince?"

The Genie smiled. That was a decent question. In truth, he *could* make Aladdin a prince, he informed him, but it was wise to be careful in the wording. As Aladdin listened, the Genie pointed out that he had, over the years, been asked the very same question—or similar ones—by countless other men. But it didn't always turn out well, because they didn't know what—or rather—*how* to ask correctly. One man told the Genie, "Make me a prince," and so the Genie did just that—literally. He made a prince *for* him. So the man ended up dragging around this royal guy. Another wisher asked to be irresistible to women. That didn't last long. Ninety seconds, to be exact.

"Moral of the story is," the Genie said when he had finished his warning, "be very specific with your words. You want to *become* a prince." He gave Aladdin a serious look. "Hold on. If she already likes you, you sure you want to go—"

"She has to marry a prince," Aladdin said, cutting him off. He had heard the warnings and it didn't matter. He knew what he wanted, what he needed. If he was going to have the power of a genie behind him, he might as well use it to his advantage.

The Genie nodded. "All right," he said. "I can do that. You just gotta phrase it as an official wish for those keeping count, which I, from now on, am." He gave Aladdin a stern glare.

Aladdin smiled sheepishly. He deserved the look. Taking a deep breath, he looked straight at the Genie. "I wish—"

"Lamp!" the Genie interrupted, pointing to Aladdin's empty hands.

"Sorry, right," Aladdin apologized. Grabbing the lamp from the ground, he took another deep breath. Then he began to rub its brass sides. As the metal warmed under his touch, Aladdin felt a shiver of fear. What if whatever the Genie did hurt? Or worse, what if he ended up like one of those guys who didn't say the right thing? Or even worse, what if he became a prince and Jasmine didn't want anything to do with him? He shook his head, chasing away the doubts. He had to find out one way or another. He had nothing to lose. "Genie," he said. "I wish to become . . . a prince."

The Genie smiled. "I'm going to need some room to work," he said.

Before Aladdin could ask why, the sand, the sun, and everything around him disappeared in a puff of blue smoke.

Chapter
Twelve

Jasmine stood in the doorway to her father's inner sanctum, watching the Sultan for a moment. Unaware he was being observed, the older man sat at his desk. In his hands he held a piece of paper, worn thin from many readings. He sighed, his eyes welling with emotion as his fingers traced the writing. It was one of the last letters Jasmine's mother had ever written to him.

Watching him, Jasmine felt a familiar tug on her heart. Her mother had been the rock upon which she and her father had relied. Her untimely death had broken their hearts and left them adrift. Neither had been comfortable seeking solace from the other, so they'd each grieved alone. For Jasmine, her grief had turned outward, and she'd channeled her energy into learning about her kingdom. For the Sultan, the grief had turned inward, and he had shut others out, trusting the day-to-day ruling to Jafar.

In Jasmine's opinion, that had been a terrible mistake.

A mistake she would very much like to remedy.

"Baba," Jasmine said softly, so as not to startle her father. The Sultan looked up as she entered the room. Raja walked in right behind her, the big cat completely comfortable and at ease in the sanctum. "I've been thinking," she went on. "Maybe this year we could move the Harvest Festival back outside the palace, like it used to be."

The Sultan sighed, reaching a hand down to rub Raja. The motion was well practiced, and the tiger let out a purr, pressing his body into the Sultan's leg as if he were a tiny house cat. "It's a nice thought, Jasmine," he said. "But the city is too dangerous now."

Jasmine shook her head. Her hands clenched into fists at her sides. "You should go into the city," she argued. "See what Jafar has been doing to it—" She wasn't allowed to finish.

"My sultan," the vizier himself said, entering the room and cutting her off. Behind him, Hakim followed, Iago flying in the air above. "I was delayed in the city on an urgent matter."

Jasmine narrowed her eyes at the man. "What

urgent matter?" she asked, her voice heavy with suspicion. A thought, fleeting and rather far-fetched, flashed through her mind. Had Jafar been behind the excessive number of guards who'd ended up chasing her and Aladdin? Had he somehow known it was her? Then she shook her head. She didn't want to give the vizier that much credit.

"You wouldn't understand the dangers of the city, Princess, venturing out rarely as you do," Jafar said, the condescension practically dripping off him. Then a dark look flashed in his eyes. "But, come to think of it, I did hear about a recent trip . . ."

Jasmine's heart dropped.

"What?" the Sultan said, his head whipping toward his daughter.

Jafar nodded. "Hakim spotted her out alone in the marketplace," he said.

"I have told you, you are *not* to leave this palace!" the Sultan said, all traces of docility vanishing.

Biting back a groan, Jasmine looked back and forth between her father and the vizier. How could her father be so blind? And how could the vizier have known? Even more important, how could he be so truly evil? This was *exactly* what Jafar wanted.

He wanted Jasmine trapped, the Sultan his pawn. "You have no idea what's happening out there!" Desperately, she looked to the head of the guards. At one time, it had been he, not Jafar, whom the Sultan had trusted above all others. "Hakim, tell him! Tell the Sultan what Agrabah has become. Tell him that this is not the city you grew up in."

But Hakim remained silent, Jasmine's pleas falling on deaf ears.

The Sultan, it seemed, had heard every word. But he didn't care about her protests. He was still focused on the fact that she had snuck out. "I encouraged your interest in these affairs so long as they didn't threaten your safety. But no more." He pushed the hat back on his head and puffed out his chest in a look that Jasmine knew meant business. "You are to stay within the palace walls, do you hear me?"

"I will post more guards outside the princess's chambers at once," Jafar said, not bothering to hide the pleasure the statement gave him.

Before leaving the room, Jasmine looked back over her shoulder and shot Jafar a hate-filled glance. But he didn't see it; he was already too busy conferring with the Sultan. Just before she left the inner sanctum, escorted by Hakim, she heard her father sigh. "Maybe she's right," she heard him say, and hope flared in her chest. "Maybe we've become less involved. Jasmine's intelligent, like her mother. Perhaps we could use her in our council meetings?"

Unfortunately, Jasmine never got to hear the vizier's response. But she could imagine it all too well. A few more excuses, words about women not being fit to rule, and the refrain that she had grown to hate—that they just needed to find her a prince.

They can try all they want, Jasmine thought as she followed Hakim toward her chambers, *but I am going to keep pushing them away, one by one. There is not a prince out there that I'll be willing to marry. Ever.*

Aladdin was beginning to wonder if Genie was actually all-powerful and not just all-boastful. Despite having made his wish to become a prince several minutes earlier, the Genie had seemingly yet to do anything other than ping him and Abu back and forth off several lone trees and the tent. No puffs of blue smoke. No abracadabra. No magic. And they ended up standing exactly where they had been—in the middle of the desert, the sun beating down on them.

Snapping his fingers, the Genie made an ornate mirror appear. Holding it up, he showed Aladdin his reflection. Aladdin's eyes narrowed. Apparently, the Genie actually *had* been doing something—he had been making Aladdin look like a prince. Or rather, the Genie's version of a prince. Aladdin's old clothes—the simple beige shirt and pants with the green belt and red vest he had worn for most of his life—were gone. Now he was wearing something else, but he wasn't sure what one would call it. All he could see was it involved a lot of wild colors, an over-the-top headpiece, and way too many jewels.

Seeing the unimpressed look on Aladdin's face, the Genie sighed. "Obviously a fashion fail." He held up a finger and began to pace around Aladdin, like a painter observing his subject. "I'm feeling periwinkle. No, chartreuse . . . cerise?" Another snap of his fingers and the outfit Aladdin was wearing changed. Only now, he was dressed in a vibrant outfit with a giant headpiece.

"This is a big hat!" Aladdin said, not impressed. Again.

Reluctantly, the Genie nodded. The kid was

right. It wasn't a good look. He began to snap through a dozen different outfits as Aladdin stood there, a human mannequin. "The lines are all wrong, colors clashing with skin tone, the silhouette is confused. It's not you!" As the Genie grew more and more frustrated, the outfits grew wilder until, with a shout, he threw his hands up in the air. "I know . . . It's got to be crisp, clean, classic. Neutral for the desert, ivory, beige, bone . . ." He let out a gasp as the answer came to him. "WHITE! And the crowd goes wild! The Genie is on fire, folks!" With another snap of the Genie's fingers, the clothes went through one last transformation. When it was complete, Aladdin's drab duds had been replaced by a simple white outfit, complete with a perfect-sized headpiece. For a few moments, the Genie danced around, praising his own genius. Finally, he stopped and looked over at Aladdin, who was staring at his reflection in the mirror. "So, what do you think?"

"I like it," Aladdin said, running his hands over the smooth, crisp fabric. It was comfortable, easy to move in. "I think it's me."

"Of course you like it," the Genie said with a cocky smile. "I made it."

"But won't everyone recognize me?" Aladdin said. While he wasn't disappointed in the transformation, it wasn't like the Genie had changed him completely. He had simply swapped his clothes. If anyone he knew saw him, it wouldn't be that hard to realize who he really was—or rather who he was *pretending* to be.

The Genie didn't seem worried. "No one will recognize you," he said confidently. "That's how genie magic works." He snapped his fingers, and the jewel-encrusted mirror grew bigger.

Aladdin looked at his reflection. He raised an eyebrow. The Genie was right. Somehow, he was him—but he also *wasn't* him. It was like a light had been lit within him and he was a more handsome, glowing version of the man he had been. Combined with the clothes, there was no way anyone would mistake him for the street rat Aladdin. "Who am I?" he finally asked.

"Prince Ali," the Genie answered without hesitation. Then he paused. "Of . . . Ababwa."

Aladdin cocked his head. "Is that a real place?"

"Real enough," the Genie said, shrugging.

Leaning over, he gazed into the mirror with Aladdin. "It's all about how you sell it."

Slowly, Aladdin nodded. He was starting to get it. Just pretend enough and believe enough, and he could be anyone he wanted. Seemed simple. "But what about transport?" he asked. He had seen the princes who arrived. They never just *walked* into the city.

"A prince needs transport!" the Genie agreed. "What says 'man of the people'? Something classy, understated . . ." He scanned the area, his eyes finally coming to rest on Abu. He considered the monkey for a long moment and then shrugged. The monkey would have to do. Lifting a hand into the air, the Genie finally sent a puff of smoke right at Abu. As Aladdin watched, Abu began to transform. His nose grew longer, his limbs stretched, and then his ears extended. When the smoke faded, Abu had been turned from a monkey into an elephant.

Pleased with his work, the Genie nodded. There was just one thing left to do. His prince had the clothes, and he had the ride. Now he just needed an entourage to complete the package. Raising both hands into the air, the Genie began to lift the sand around them. Blurry, indistinct shapes emerged at first; then the sand shifted and molded and became clear. First instruments, then soldiers, then finally some dancers and prancing exotic animals. It was a parade of epic and jaw-dropping scale. Just the type of parade needed for the newly crowned Prince Ali of Ababwa.

Aladdin smiled. Jasmine needed to marry a prince? Well, the Genie had made him a prince. Now he just had to convince an entire city he was worthy of that title—and, most important, Jasmine.

What Aladdin didn't know, at least not until it was too late, was that the Genie wasn't going to just make him into any prince. He was going to make him *the greatest prince of all time*. As they came closer to the city, the Genie told Aladdin of his plan to "introduce" Prince Ali to Agrabah. A plan that involved an enormous, elaborate parade, which continued to grow as they walked.

By the time they reached the outer gates of the city, Aladdin had a menagerie of seventy-five golden camels, over four dozen purple peacocks, and countless other exotic animals. All magically made, of course, and led by elephant Abu, who had seemed to embrace his new look, strutting proudly. And the animals were just a small part of the parade. There were dozens of dancing people chanting his name. There was a brass band, bakers, cooks, and even birds that warbled on cue and on key.

Bursting through the gates, the Genie disguised himself among the growing crowd of curious onlookers and spread rumors about Prince Ali's feats of strength and grand generosity. He told gaggles of woman the tales of Ali's romantic heart, and bragged to jealous men of how the prince had fought off a horde of a hundred sword-yielding marauders. All without breaking a sweat.

By the time they arrived in front of the palace itself, the whole city was abuzz and already enamored with the handsome, generous, brave, and caring Prince Ali of Ababwa.

Chapter

Thirteen

Jasmine had witnessed the arrival of Prince Ali. But unlike her people, who seemed all too eager to fall for his parade of animals and the whispered words of his fabulous deeds, Jasmine had not yet decided how she felt about the mysterious prince. She had seen men making fools of themselves before. This prince was doing no different, just doing it on a grander scale.

Following her father into the Great Hall, Jasmine took her place next to him. On his other side, Jafar sidled up, a frown on his face, Iago perched on his shoulder. Together, the trio turned to watch as the prince made his way toward them down the long hall. When he arrived, he bowed—and seemed to get stuck, hovering with his face toward the ground until his attendant nudged him. Jasmine's eyes narrowed as she watched the interplay between prince and attendant. The prince seemed oddly uncomfortable, and the attendant seemed a tad . . . blue.

"It's a pleasure to welcome you to Agrabah, Prince Ali," the Sultan said in greeting after the excessive bowing was complete.

"I'm as . . . pleasured as you are, sir," the prince stammered. "Sir, Your Highness, sir."

Jasmine couldn't help smiling. There was something oddly charming about the bumbling prince. Jafar, however, did not seem to feel the same way. He stepped forward, eyeing the newcomer suspiciously. "I'm afraid I'm unfamiliar with Ababwa," he said. Iago flew over and pecked at the prince's hat.

"It's north," the prince's attendant said, while at the same time, Prince Ali said, "It's south." Jasmine saw him shoot the attendant a look. "It has a north *and* a south," he corrected.

"The world is changing so quickly," the Sultan said, ignoring the prince's odd answer and his vizier's suspicion. He had been quite taken by Prince Ali and his parade and wanted to give the young—and rather impressive—man a chance to woo his daughter. "It seems as if there's a new country every day."

Aladdin nodded. But then he just stood there.

An awkward silence stretched over the Great Hall. Jasmine watched as once again the prince and his attendant exchanged pointed looks. Then the attendant cleared his throat and hissed, in a barely veiled whisper, "Tell him you brought some gifts."

"Oh! Right! We brought things. Gifts." On cue, a line of servants stepped forward and began to present items to the Sultan and Jasmine. "We've got . . . silk . . . and spices . . . and spoons. Tiny spoons. Some jams?"

"Jams?" Jafar repeated.

The prince flushed several shades of red and looked over at his attendant with an expression that screamed *Help me!* Not receiving any assistance, however, he shrugged and then nodded. "Yam jams, fig jams, seedless jams . . ." His voice trailed off as he was apparently unable to think of any more.

Jasmine once again bit back a laugh. This prince was the oddest one she had ever met. It seemed like he had never presented a gift in his life. And from the way he was eyeing the spices and decadent food with apparent hunger, it also seemed like he hadn't eaten anything in a while.

Shifting on his feet, Prince Ali continued his

presentation. Jasmine waited. He might not be acting like a prince, but he was one nevertheless, which meant sooner or later he was going to present her with some jewels or some over-the-top present to try to woo her and win her heart. Sure enough, as if on cue, he pointed to one of the items now being offered.

"I don't know what that is," he said, "but I bet it's expensive."

"And what do you hope to buy with this 'expensive' thing?" Jasmine asked. Behind her, she heard Dalia give a little snort. The handmaiden knew exactly what Jasmine was doing.

Prince Ali, however, walked right into her trap. Looking up, he blushed. "You," he said. His cheeks grew still more crimson. "I mean . . . a moment with you?"

Jasmine raised one perfectly sculpted eyebrow. "Are you suggesting I am for sale?"

"No!" the prince exclaimed, looking mortified. "I . . . no . . ."

Jasmine didn't allow him to continue. Flicking her long, thick dark braid over her shoulder, she turned and began to stride down the hall, leaving the men behind. Dalia followed, but not before throwing the prince's attendant an interested look.

"Er, that's . . . not what I meant," Jasmine heard the prince say as she walked away. Her stride faltered and for the tiniest of moments she thought of turning back. But then her father spoke for her.

"Don't worry," the Sultan said. "You'll have a chance to speak again. We hope you'll join us tonight, Prince Ali, when we celebrate our harvest."

Jasmine didn't hear the prince's response. All she could hear was the angry pounding of her heart as once more she became a pawn in a political game. A game she had no chance of winning. A game that gave her no chance of anything.

Aladdin stared out the window of the guest chambers, oblivious to his opulent and luxurious surroundings. All he could think of was how royally he had messed up his first meeting with Jasmine as Prince Ali. It could not have gone any worse. He let out a groan and reached up, throwing his headpiece to the ground.

Behind him, he heard the giggles of several

servant girls as they attempted to offer him a snack. But they were met by the Genie instead. "Thank you, so kind," he said, looking at the scrumptious trays. "But someone's been a really naughty boy and doesn't deserve any of this. So thank you, ladies, bye-bye."

Aladdin turned around just in time to see them—and the food—walk out the door. "I'm hungry!' he said, hearing the whine in his own voice. Abu, a monkey once more, added his own protest, chittering angrily and raising his little hand to point after the food.

The Genie looked over at Aladdin and raised an eyebrow. "'And what do you intend to buy with this expensive thing?' 'You!'" he said, repeating the painfully awkward conversation.

"That was a misunderstanding," Aladdin said, but his words sounded hollow. They both knew it hadn't just been a misunderstanding. It had been a disaster.

"You made me look like a bad genie," the Genie said, agreeing with Aladdin's thoughts. "If I had known you were this bad with women, I would have rethought the strategy, done something where you didn't talk."

"Well . . ." Aladdin said, trying to think of how he could defend himself.

The Genie's eyebrows magically rose off his face. Then he shook his head. "You've said enough for today. Now you've got one more chance tonight at this party. But I need you to go sit in the corner and marinate on round two." The Genie pointed to the far corner of the tower. Then he flopped down on a long chaise and stretched out. "I'm going to lay here, close my eyes, and forget the tragedy of the afternoon."

His assumed a resting position. But he sat up a moment later as outside, fireworks began to explode in the sky. "Ooh!" the Genie cried. "I love fireworks. Nothing better than a party. Let's go . . ."

Aladdin nodded. It was now or never. He was going to show Jasmine that he was still *him*—just better. He was going to pick up where they had left off before, find that spark and connection that had come so easily when he had just been Aladdin.

He just didn't quite know how. . . .

Luckily, the Genie wasn't going to stand by and let him flail around like a drowning bug. He announced they had some quick training to do—in the art of talking and wooing a princess. As the fireworks continued to explode, they practiced opening lines and easy ways to jump-start a conversation. The Genie made books appear out of thin air so that Aladdin could read about what was happening in the world. "She'll like a prince who knows something," the Genie said. "Trust me." And when the learning portion of the training was over, Aladdin allowed himself to be dressed and primped and perfected, so by the time they finally went down to the Harvest Festival, Aladdin felt like his skin had been sandblasted, his hair had been pulled out, and his eyes were on fire. But at least he looked royal. Or so the Genie told him.

They headed out of the guest chambers and toward the festivities. Walking into the palace courtyard, Aladdin took a deep breath. For the first time that day, he stopped and allowed himself to look around. Really look around. The night sky was cloudless, stars twinkling brightly, the moon hanging directly above as if it were the palace's personal chandelier. Partygoers dressed in brilliant colors, jewels glittering on their hands and around their throats, wandered under fragrant blooms and past exotic birds. It was the most beautiful thing Aladdin had ever seen.

And then he turned and saw Jasmine.

His jaw dropped.

His heart began to pound.

His palms grew sweaty.

And he was pretty sure he wanted to throw up.

The palace and the grounds paled in comparison to the beauty of Jasmine. She looked like something from his dreams. Her turquoise outfit—complete with a peacock motif on her trousers and sheer cape—sparkled and shone as she began to move through the party, catching the light from the moon above and the candles on the tables. Following Aladdin's gaze, the Genie let out a low whistle.

"Here's your opening," he said. But then his own eyes widened as he spotted Dalia—the *real* Dalia. "That little handmaiden is a bit of a treat herself, eyes the color of oolong tea—" He stopped, noticing Aladdin staring at him with an amused expression. "She's going to get punch. I feel a little thirsty myself—"

Aladdin's expression changed from amused to terrified. He began to shake his head frantically.

"No," he said, clutching at the collar of the Genie's shirt. "Don't leave. They'll see through me!"

The Genie pulled Aladdin's fingers off his collar one by one. "No, they won't. All you have to do is go over there."

"And speak. I'll also have to sp—" Aladdin began to protest. But it was too late. The Genie was already slipping away through the crowd, making a beeline for Dalia. Aladdin sighed. It looked like he had no choice but to go for it on his own.

Okay, he thought, trying to muster up his courage. *You can do this. Genie believes in you. You've just got to go up to her and say hi. No big deal. You've talked to her before. . . .*

Taking a deep breath, Aladdin started over. But at that exact moment, Prince Anders did the same. Instantly, Aladdin spun on his heels. It was one thing to try and get Jasmine's attention when it was just him. But to try and fight for her attention with Prince Anders? No way. The guy was pure Nordic perfection. Next to him, Aladdin's lack of princely experience would be even more noticeable.

"How's anyone supposed to compete with that?" Aladdin said as the Genie came back over, a glass of punch in his hand. "He's so tall, so princely."

Together, they watched as Prince Anders engaged Jasmine in conversation. He was holding something up for Jasmine to look at. Squinting, Aladdin tried to see what it was, but he couldn't quite figure it out. It looked like a pen. Or maybe a fork? Whatever it was, Jasmine seemed intrigued, letting out a laugh.

"That goofy man?" the Genie said. "He wears a fur hat in the desert. You gotta be more confident in what you have to offer." He clapped Aladdin on the back. Then he pointed to himself. "Look at me. Do you see how I own my walk? I don't even have legs!"

But Aladdin was still staring at the prince and princess. His frowned deepened. "What do I have to offer? She has a tiger, I have a monkey. She has this palace." He shook his head. "That Ali, he does have a lot of jewels—"

The Genie shook his head. "Not Ali, *you*," he corrected. "I made you look like a prince. I didn't change what's on offer on the inside. Prince Ali got you to the door, but *Aladdin* has the key to opening it. Trust yourself."

Aladdin looked over at the Genie. Trust himself? This was the opportunity of a lifetime — one he'd longed for. But on the inside, he couldn't help feeling that he was still a street rat. The Genie hadn't done any more to change him than give him a title and an entourage. He hadn't taught him how to be a prince or act like he had been born into royalty. Aladdin didn't even know how to do a proper bow! He still barely believed what had happened. The man who stared back at him in the mirror felt like a stranger. How was he going to convince others that he was a prince? What chance did he have to make anyone like him, let alone make Jasmine *love* him? Dragging his attention away from where the princess continued to talk to Anders, Aladdin locked eyes with the Sultan. The older man raised his glass in salute. At least the Sultan seemed to like him.

Suddenly, Aladdin felt the Genie grab his arm and begin pulling him across the courtyard — straight toward Jasmine, who was now unoccupied as Prince Anders seemed to be regaling a crowd of admirers. Protesting under his breath, Aladdin tried to wrench his arm free. But it was no use. The Genie was strong, *all-powerful-being* strong.

"Okay, lover boy, time is now," the Genie said, brushing off Aladdin's attempts to struggle away like the young man was nothing more than an annoying bug. "No more waiting."

"No," Aladdin said, shaking his head weakly. "I'm in charge. I'll say when it's the right time—" But he didn't have a chance to finish before the Genie shoved him, rather unceremoniously, right in front of Jasmine. Looking up, Aladdin gulped. "Um, hello," he said awkwardly.

Jasmine raised an eyebrow. "Hello."

Awkward silence fell between them. Aladdin shuffled nervously while Jasmine crossed her arms and waited. Clearly, she was expecting Prince Ali to say something. But Aladdin's mind had gone blank. Up close Jasmine was even more beautiful, and it was like his brain had switched off. All he could do was stand there, his jaw slack and his brain empty. Hearing a loud throat-clearing sound from behind him, courtesy of the Genie, Aladdin finally shook himself free of his stupor. "Sorry for earlier," he began. "I didn't mean to . . . I'm not really used to partying. I mean, I am, but . . ."

"Dance?" Jasmine asked, stopping him before he could dig himself a deeper hole. "I'd love to."

Holding out her hand, she waited for Aladdin to take it.

Aladdin's heart swelled in gratitude. He wiped his suddenly clammy palm against his pant leg and took her hand in his. Then he allowed her to lead him out onto the dance floor. His mind had suddenly gone back to blank. Dance? With Jasmine? He was going to make a total fool of himself. He had never danced in his life, let alone danced with a princess. Shooting a desperate look in the Genie's direction, he felt a rush of magic and then his legs began to move of their own accord. As the music grew louder and faster, his legs and arms moved faster and faster, making him look like a flailing puppet and causing Jasmine to laugh out loud.

Her laughter, kind and full of life, surprised Aladdin. Meeting her eyes, he was surprised to see softness. A wave of confidence washed over him. He sent the Genie another look. But this time, it didn't scream, *Help me!* Instead, it said, *I've got this.*

As the beat of the music grew louder, Aladdin let himself go. He stopped thinking about the people watching him. He stopped caring about the looks he felt on his back. He stopped wondering if anyone could tell he was a fake. He didn't even try to follow the steps of the dance, like everyone else. All he did was focus on the sound of Jasmine's laughter and the feel of her hand in his and the pleasure it gave him. Their eyes met, and they shared a smile.

Emboldened, Aladdin spun Jasmine out and then pulled her back in to him. The audience, warmed over by the obvious fun the pair was having, let out a round of applause. Aladdin grinned. *I've totally got this,* he thought. *Why did I even worry?* Spinning Jasmine again, he moved his feet in an elaborate—and made up—series of steps. Then he shook his head and moved his shoulders up and down. Caught up in the adoration of the crowd and his own moves, he completely missed Jasmine as she spun back toward him. She sailed past him, coming to a stop with a confused look on her face.

Aladdin barely noticed. He was having too much fun now. It was nice to be the center of attention. Or rather, the center of attention *in a good way* for once. Not the focus of a chase through the streets. He looked over at Jasmine. To his surprise, her look of confusion had morphed into one of sadness. She pulled back and left the dance floor.

"Wait—" Aladdin called. But it was too late.

Jasmine had already disappeared into the palace. Aladdin sighed. He had ruined the moment. He had gotten so caught up in showing off that he hadn't even thought about Jasmine. Which, he realized as the dancers around him crowded closer, was probably exactly what every other prince had ever done to her.

I was supposed to show her I was different, Aladdin thought as he left the dance floor himself. *And all I did was show her I'm just as big a jerk as Prince Anders. How am I ever going to make her see who I really am now?*

Heading toward the guest chambers, lost in his worries, Aladdin didn't notice Jafar's suspicious eyes on him. Nor did he hear the flapping of wings as Iago took to the air at his master's orders to follow the new prince. . . .

Chapter

Fourteen

Back in his chambers, Aladdin once again found himself staring out the large windows. If he leaned out far enough and craned his head slightly to the right, he could just make out the edge of Jasmine's quarters in the far tower. He wondered what she was doing. Was she wishing she had never met Prince Ali? Was she mocking him? Cursing his name? He let out another deep sigh. He had messed things up—royally.

"Abu, I've seen what you do with your monkey fingers. Will you please get them out of my house?"

The Genie's voice startled Aladdin and he turned. A smile spread across his face. Abu was holding on to the lamp, a guilty expression on his face as the Genie stared at him, arms crossed angrily. Slowly, Abu lowered the lamp to the ground and then held up his hands in surrender. Satisfied he was not going to be changed into any other creature, he turned his back on the Genie and began to annoy the carpet.

Watching the two bicker, Aladdin felt a wave of frustration wash over him. "If I had just had a few more minutes with her," Aladdin said, looking back out the window. Then his eyes narrowed. He turned and looked at the Genie. "You have to get me over there."

"Is that an official wish?" the Genie asked.

Aladdin shook his head. "No," he answered. "It's a favor. For a friend."

The Genie looked surprised. "Genies don't really have those. When you're a genie, someone always wants something. . . . It's awkward."

Aladdin nodded. That made sense. But at the same time, he couldn't just give up. Not when he had gotten this close and blown it over a few silly dance moves. He needed to see Jasmine, one way or another. The Genie had to understand that. . . . Suddenly, Aladdin smiled. Come to think of it, he was pretty sure the Genie knew *exactly* what it was like to be interested in someone. "That favor," he said, trying again. "It would involve distracting Jasmine's handmaiden . . ."

He didn't need to finish. "I'll meet you there,"

the Genie said. And then, before Aladdin could even say thanks, he poofed away in a swirl of blue smoke.

Aladdin smiled.

Jasmine was tired. Another night, another dance, another prince, another failure. When would it ever end? She had thought, hoped, for a brief moment that Prince Ali might be different. There had been something about him, something free and unrestrained, that had flared a feeling of possibility within her. He had seemed the kind of person who might see that she was capable of being so much more than just a pretty face. He had seemed to be someone who might see that she could be a ruler, a voice for her people.

And then he had gone and acted like a typical pompous prince.

Hearing a knock at the door, Jasmine didn't even bother to turn around. She knew Dalia would answer it and send whoever it was away. Moving out onto the balcony, she stared down at the city below. It was a peaceful evening, a soft breeze carrying the smell of flowers. Behind her, she heard the heavy doors swing open. Then she heard the sound of Prince Ali's attendant.

"Good evening," he said.

Jasmine turned but stayed hidden in the shadows. She could see Ali's attendant clearly. The handsome man was leaning against the door, his arms crossed over his muscular chest. Tall and broad, he seemed to fill the doorway.

"How did you get past the guards?" Dalia asked.

"Sort of snuck past," the man answered.

"All forty-eight of them, even the ones that eat fire? Impressive," Dalia said, her answer making Jasmine smile. She, like Jasmine, had heard it all before. Although Jasmine had to think that Dalia had probably never heard it from an attendant quite as handsome as this one.

Unable to stop herself, Jasmine turned around to watch the two of them. She knew Dalia well enough to know that while she was feigning indifference, she wasn't blind to the man's charms—or his good looks.

He lifted a bouquet of flowers and held them out.

"Beautiful!" Dalia said, graciously taking

them. Then she frowned. "She'll hate them. Tell Prince Ali the way to her heart is through her mind. Poetry, philosophy . . ."

The attendant stared at Dalia. He looked truly mystified by her response. Jasmine found herself taking a step closer, curious to hear what the attendant would say—or offer. But to her surprise, he shook his head. "Actually," he said, pointing at the flowers, "these are for you, from me."

Jasmine's breath caught. She had *not* seen that coming. But her heart swelled suddenly for her handmaiden and friend. There was something so romantic about the attendant's surprise arrival. And Dalia seemed to think the same thing. Turning around, she searched the room for Jasmine. Once she caught sight of the princess, she silently let out a scream of glee. Then, regaining her composure, she turned back to the attendant. "I accept, thank you." She lifted the flowers to her nose and took a dainty sniff. "What else?"

"A stroll," the man said. "Would you like to go on an evening stroll?"

"Just the two of us? On purpose?" she asked.

He nodded.

And then she slammed the door in his face.

Jasmine smiled as she watched Dalia race around the room, grabbing a fresh wrap from the large wardrobe and throwing it over her shoulders. Taking a quick look in the mirror, she brushed wisps of hair out of her face and then bit her lips, making them redden. With a nod to Jasmine, who was now laughing, Dalia walked back to the door and swung it open.

"My answer is yes," she said.

As Jasmine hid in the shadows, Prince Ali's perplexed attendant smiled broadly and let out a happy, "Yes!" Then, holding out his arm for Dalia, he escorted her from the chambers. Jasmine watched them go, a pang of jealousy hitting her. She would have loved for someone to come and ask to take her on a stroll. Such a simple request, but one that would mean more than all the fancy gifts in the world.

Suddenly, there was the sound of another knock. "Come in . . ." Jasmine said absently, confident it was just Dalia returning to grab something before her romantic stroll.

"I'm in already."

At the sound of Prince Ali's voice, Raja began

to snarl, and Jasmine whipped around. A moment later, the prince stepped out of the shadows and into the moonlight flooding the balcony.

Jasmine's heart slammed against her chest. How had he gotten up there? She looked around, but saw no ladder, no obvious rope hanging from a higher window. She shook her head. "Don't move!" she ordered as her large tiger's protective snarls grew louder.

"I won't," the prince said. "I just came because you left so abruptly."

Jasmine narrowed her eyes. Was he implying she should feel bad for leaving him in the middle of his one-man dance show? Well, if he was looking for an apology, he was going to be standing there for a while. Jasmine tried not to be distracted by the way the moonlight highlighted the prince's cheekbones and made his thick, dark hair shine. Or the way his eyes sparkled with kindness. She focused her thoughts. She *had* actually been hoping to see him again. Since she had left the festival, something had been nagging at her. Finally, she shrugged. "Actually, now that you're here, I can't seem to find Ababwa on any of my maps. Can you show me?" She walked over to a table in her chambers and pointed to the pile of maps spread over it.

"Am I allowed to move?" the prince asked, looking over at Raja, who immediately snarled.

"Raja, don't eat the prince," Jasmine said. "He needs his legs for dancing."

The prince's cheeks flushed and he looked down, embarrassed. "Did I go too far?"

"A little," Jasmine said, though her tone implied it was far more than a little. She pointed back at the maps. "So . . . Ababwa."

Walking over, Prince Ali looked down at the maps. He began to trace one, his finger running over the countries outlined below. He shifted uncomfortably on his feet and she could swear she saw his lips moving, as if he were mumbling to himself. Her eyebrows arched. Why was he acting so strange? Had he lost his country? Or was she correct and there was no Ababwa after all? But then he smiled and jabbed his finger to a spot on the map. "See! There it is!"

Jasmine frowned. It was impossible. She had looked over every inch of every map. There had been no Ababwa. Leaning over, she looked at where Ali was pointing. Her eyes narrowed further. She still didn't see anything. But then she blinked and shook her head as, suddenly, under his finger, a country seemed to appear. And in the middle, in ink faded with time, was the name ABABWA. "How did I not see that?" she said finally.

Prince Ali shrugged. "Maps are old and useless, with no practical value."

"Maps are the way I see the world," Jasmine replied, more bitterly than she would have liked.

"Really?" Ali said. "I'd think a princess would go everywhere." He sounded like he was sincerely trying to make amends for putting his foot in his mouth, and Jasmine felt her anger begin to soften.

Sighing, she walked away from the maps and back onto the balcony. "Not this princess," she said softly.

Hearing his footsteps behind her, Jasmine turned and saw the prince lean against one of the short pillars that served as decorations for her chamber. On top of it was a bowl of pomegranates. As Ali's weight pressed fully upon the pillar, it began to wobble. The bowl, unsettled by the motion, began to fall, and just before the pomegranates hit the floor, Ali reached out and caught three of them. The fourth landed on the ground and rolled toward Jasmine's feet.

"Oops," the prince said. Reaching down, he grabbed it and threw it, along with the fruit he had successfully caught, back into the bowl. As he did so, Raja walked over and licked his face. The prince looked as surprised as Jasmine felt. But then he smiled and gave the big tiger a pat. "Thanks for that, I needed a face wash."

As Jasmine watched her large and protective tiger rub up against the prince like he recognized an old friend, she couldn't help smiling. The initial melting continued, and she felt a strange surge of compassion for the prince, even a bit of affection. Her tiger had never approved of any of her suitors. Frankly, he had taken years to even warm up to Dalia. Yet there he was, acting like a lap cat with this stranger. She didn't understand, but she didn't hate it, either. In fact, Jasmine found it endearing. There was something rather charming about this prince. And while he apparently *was* a prince from an actual country, there was something refreshingly unprincely about him.

Sensing her eyes on him, the prince looked over. "Um, I was saying," Ali went on, looking up from the tiger, "we should go see these places. There's a whole world outside of books. Do you want to?"

"How?" Jasmine asked. "Every door is guarded."

The prince smiled, his eyes lighting up. "Who said anything about a door?"

Jasmine watched as, keeping his gaze on her, he began to back toward the edge of the balcony. She opened her mouth to warn him, but to her surprise, the prince jumped up onto the balcony railing. He gave her a huge smile.

And then, he jumped.

Chapter

Fifteen

Aladdin heard Jasmine's gasp. He felt the wind in his hair and on his cheeks. He felt warm air beneath him. For one long moment, he simply fell.

Until, with a whoosh, the carpet flew up from beneath him and caught him. Aladdin's feet settled onto the rug, the pace of his plummet slowing and then reversing as the carpet lifted him back up to the balcony. He put his hands on his hips and stood still as the carpet continued to float up, until he was standing face-to-face with the princess.

Her eyes were wide and her hand was at her heart. Aladdin allowed himself a moment of hope that perhaps she had been worried about him, but then she pointed to the carpet. "What is that?" she asked breathlessly.

"Magic carpet," Aladdin said, as though a flying carpet were something one saw every day.

In the moonlight, with curiosity in her eyes

and her cheeks flushed with excitement, Jasmine was more beautiful than ever. In that moment, Aladdin wanted nothing more than to tell her who he was, admit what he had done, and hope she would see that he had done it out of, dare he say . . . love. But he knew it was too soon. He didn't need the Genie to tell him that. So instead, he held out his hand. "Do you trust me?" he asked. As the words left his mouth, Aladdin nearly groaned. That was exactly what he had said to her back in the market.

"What did you say?" Jasmine asked. Her eyes met his, and she looked searchingly at him. Her hand began to lift toward his face, her fingers reaching . . .

Not giving the princess a chance to put two and two together, Aladdin closed his hand around hers and pulled her onto the carpet with him. Together, they sat down, the air between them charged with unspoken emotion as the carpet began to fly them away from the palace and out over Agrabah. The city soon grew smaller, becoming a collage of shining, shimmering buildings. Over clouds and then beside them, the carpet glided. Sitting there, next to a breathless Jasmine, Aladdin felt a freedom greater than any he had known. He couldn't imagine what

Jasmine was thinking. Her life, she had told him, was dictated by her father and his rules. He wondered when the last time was that she had done something just because she dreamed of doing it.

Opening his mouth to ask her, he stopped as he caught sight of the wonder written all over her face. Clearly, she was feeling the same way he was—as though she were seeing the world for the first time. Dragging his attention from her beauty, Aladdin watched as the clouds raced by, imagining them as mythical beasts or boats sailing over the seas. The carpet dipped back down toward the ground, and Aladdin saw that they were now out over the wide-open desert. Riding aboard a magic carpet with the stars above them, they saw the desert become a place of beauty and abundance, not the dry and dull landscape it appeared to be during the day. Grabbing Jasmine's hand, he pointed to a herd of wild horses racing across the dunes. A smile lit up her face as she saw one of the younger foals throw back its head and let out a surprised whinny at the carpet.

As they dropped down closer still, Jasmine's eyes snapped shut. Reaching over, Aladdin put a finger below her chin and lifted her face to his. "Open your eyes; don't miss it," he whispered. She nodded as she slowly, and somewhat reluctantly, moved her face from Aladdin's touch. Together, they turned their attention back to the magical ride. They left the desert and flew over snowcapped mountains, then down into lush jungles. Over wide seas where dolphins played and then back up into the clouds to chase a flock of birds. For hours they flew, until finally, the unfamiliar and thrilling worlds they had seen disappeared, replaced with the more familiar desert and then, at last, the outline of Agrabah. Cresting over one of the far walls, they flew over a wedding, dozens of burning candles and lanterns causing the whole place to glow.

"Of all the places you've shown me," Jasmine said, indicating the Agrabah skyline, "this is by far the most beautiful."

Aladdin nodded. "Sometimes you just have to see it from a different perspective," he said. He looked down and watched as the bride and groom danced beneath the candlelight, lost in each other's eyes.

Following his gaze, Jasmine smiled. "It's them, the people," she offered. "They make it beautiful. And they deserve a leader who knows that. I don't know why I believe it could be me, but I do."

"Because it should be you." Aladdin was surprised by the boldness of his response. It had been that way since he'd first met Jasmine—he felt a sort of comfort and ease, as if they had known each other for a long time. He had spent so many years alone, with only Abu for company, that he had forgotten what it was like to see someone and, in turn, be truly seen by them. And he saw Jasmine. He knew how she felt. How trapped by her circumstances she must be. "You have the strength, the mind, and the courage."

Jasmine let out a sigh. "You think so?"

"Does it matter what I think?" He stopped and smiled at her, realizing the mood had shifted.

To his surprise, Jasmine didn't answer right away. Instead, she grew silent. Her eyes narrowed. She leaned in closer. For one heart-pounding moment, Aladdin thought maybe she was going to kiss him. But then she snapped back and looked down at the market below. "Look at that cute little monkey down there. Is that Abu?"

Without thinking, Aladdin shook his head. "No, it couldn't be Abu. He's still—" Aladdin's mouth snapped shut.

But it was too late. Jasmine had caught him.

"I knew it was you!" she cried.

Jasmine clapped her hands together, pleased to have discovered the truth. She had suspected something was off from the first moment she met Prince Ali. And then when he had been so strange on the dance floor. And the familiar expression he had used on the balcony. All the pieces had been there, she just hadn't put them together. Until now.

"*Who* is Prince Ali?" she asked, eager for answers now that she was out of the dark.

"I am," the young man said quickly. "I . . . like to . . . go among the people. So I can . . . know those I wish to govern."

Jasmine wasn't buying it. She had followed him through the city, watched as he navigated the streets and rooftops like he had done it dozens of times before. He had been as familiar with the market as she was with her chambers, had known the people like she knew Dalia. Her eyes narrowed. "How could you know the city so well?"

She waited and watched the prince's face, looking for any sign that he was lying to her. But his expression remained unreadable. "I came to Agrabah early," he answered. "If you want to know a people, you have to see them for yourself." He stopped, and his eyes warmed. "But you know this. When I met you, you were disguised in your own city."

Her cheeks flushed. He *did* have a point. But that had been a onetime attempt. From the sound of it, Prince Ali did this often.

"But . . . how did I not recognize you?" Her eyes traveled up the length of his white pants and vest, the cloth rich and without a speck of dirt on it. His thick hair gleamed in the moonlight, and on his wrists, gold bands sparkled. When she had met him as Aladdin, he had been covered in the dust of the streets, his hair a mess and his only accessory a worn brown bag. He had looked like every other street rat she had wandered by in the market.

Ali had another answer at the ready. "People don't see the real you when you are royalty."

Jasmine slowly nodded. Everything he said made sense. Everything he said made him seem like the type of prince she *would* want to marry—if she ever agreed to marry anybody, that is. He was a man who cared about his people. The type of guy who wanted to know what it was like on the streets, not just sit in his palace and let others dictate the lives of those he ruled. She began to shake her head, embarrassed. She had been wrong to not trust him. "You saw more of Agrabah in days than I have in a lifetime," she finally said, allowing her voice to completely soften and her stiff shoulders to loosen.

Jasmine lowered her eyes. She didn't want him to see how she didn't want the night to end. He had, she thought, shown her more than she could have imagined. He had made her realize that she *could* feel something, that there *could* be a way to marry a prince and not be miserable. Feeling his gaze on her, Jasmine looked up at the prince. For a long moment, they both just stood there, unsure of what was happening between them.

"We should probably get back," the prince finally said, breaking the moment. "It's nearly morning."

"Already?" Jasmine replied softly.

Nodding, Aladdin pointed to the horizon. The sun was just beginning to peek over, illuminating the palace. Jasmine knew he was right. She had to get back to her chambers before her father, or worse the vizier, awoke. The prince, reading her face, quickly gave the carpet a quick pat. The carpet, who had been hovering above the city, slowly began to make its way back to the balcony of Jasmine's chambers.

Once they arrived, it softly set her down, and the prince stood up on it, perfectly balanced.

"See you later, Princess?" he asked hopefully.

Jasmine nodded and smiled. She waved good-bye as the carpet began to sink beneath the railing. Unable to help herself, and hopeful that perhaps the prince was still looking up, she ran to the edge and peered over. Suddenly, the carpet floated back up. Before she knew what was happening, she felt the prince's lips on hers. A gasp of surprise caught in her throat as she let herself melt into Prince Ali.

And then, just like that, the carpet floated away, breaking them apart.

Jasmine watched him go, a finger on her lips. That had been, she thought, as the carpet and the prince disappeared from view, the perfect night—and the perfect kiss.

Chapter
Sixteen

I t had been, hands down, the best night of his
life. Aladdin could still feel Jasmine's lips on
his, could still smell the lavender in her hair
and feel her hand next to his as they flew over cities
and oceans. He was pretty sure that in the history
of evenings, they had just had the best one ever.

He just wished it never had to end.

As the carpet flew to the window of the guest
tower and deposited Aladdin in the middle of the
large chamber, Aladdin hummed under his breath.
He swooned around the room, unaware that the
carpet, Abu, and Genie were all watching him,
amused.

"Good date?" the Genie asked.

"The best," Aladdin said. Suddenly, he
frowned, and his eyes narrowed as he looked over
at the Genie. "But she figured out I was Aladdin!
You said that wouldn't happen!"

Genie shrugged. "Genie magic is just a facade,"

he said nonchalantly. "At some point, real character's always going to shine through. That's a good thing. Now she knows."

"Eventually I'll tell her the truth," Aladdin replied vaguely. "Anyway, I sort of *am* a prince now . . ."

"You're going to drink from that cup?" the Genie asked, eyebrow raised and disappointment on his face.

Aladdin shifted uncomfortably on his feet. He still felt bad about lying to Jasmine. But when she had found him out, he'd panicked. He had just stuck with the story because it seemed easier than trying to explain everything about the lamp, and Genie, and wishes. He hadn't wanted to dig himself a deeper hole, but he hadn't seen another way out.

Feeling the Genie's eyes on him, Aladdin shrugged. He had beat himself up enough about not being entirely truthful. He didn't need to stick around the room and have the Genie and Abu, and even the carpet, do the same. Waving a hand in the air, he made his way to leave. Though it was clear from Abu's chittering that he agreed with the Genie's sentiments, he was still a loyal friend, and he hopped on Aladdin's shoulder before the door could close. Together, the two of them began to walk aimlessly down the palace's corridors, taking a left here, a right there. Neither had any sense of where they were, but Aladdin didn't care. His head was back in the clouds, his heart and soul on the carpet with Jasmine as they explored a whole new world together.

Coming to the end of one particularly long corridor, Aladdin was pleased to find himself looking out into the courtyard. Maybe, if he was lucky, he would catch a glimpse of Jasmine. His pace quickened at the thought and he burst into the open courtyard, the wind warm on his cheeks, the air fragrant. He began to hum a tune, enjoying the peaceful beauty, his fingers trailing along the exotic plants.

And then, he heard the sound of heavy footsteps. Lots of heavy footsteps.

Looking up, Aladdin saw a group of Jafar's guards approaching him. He stopped, the dreadfully familiar shadows blocking his light. "Not again," he muttered under his breath. He gave a quick nod to Abu, and the monkey jumped down and quickly hid himself from view. When he was sure his friend was safe, Aladdin turned and waited for the guards to approach. From their grim demeanor, he was certain they weren't just coming to say hello.

He was right. Grabbing him roughly by the arms, one of the men threw a bag over his head. Then, before he could mutter a protest, he felt his legs go out from underneath him as he was unceremoniously dragged away. He desperately tried to keep track of the turns they made and the number of stairs he was brought up and down and then up again. But after a while, he lost count. By the time he heard a door creak open, his head was hanging low, his arms numb and his legs bruised.

A moment later, he was shoved into a chair and wrapped in what felt like very large, very painful chains. Then the bag was ripped off his head.

Standing in front of him, his arms crossed and his pesky parrot on his shoulder, was Jafar. And he did not look happy. He stepped forward, the guards moving away to give him a clearer path to Aladdin.

"Hey, hold on," Aladdin said, shifting uncomfortably on the chair. "I think you're confused . . . I don't think you know who I am."

"Oh, shut up," Jafar snapped. "I know who you are . . . Aladdin."

Aladdin gulped. The man was nothing if not perceptive. But he couldn't just give in. "Aladdin?" he said, shaking his head and trying to look perplexed. "No, I'm Prince Ali of Ababwa."

"A prince from a kingdom that doesn't exist, who now possesses a magic carpet from the Cave of Wonders?" Jafar shook his head. "It seems to me the only way *that's* possible is if you found a certain treasure—*my* treasure. Where is the lamp?"

Jafar wasn't the first nasty guy Aladdin had had to deal with, so he figured he would just do what he did on the streets—improvise. "I don't know what you're talking about." he said, feigning ignorance.

Striding over, Jafar leaned down and lifted Aladdin's head so they were eye to eye. "I have to say, I'm impressed," he said, his breath hot on Aladdin's cheek. "I didn't think you had it in you. I admire your ambition. The challenge is, it conflicts with my own."

"There's clearly some misunderstanding," Aladdin said, still trying to play the part of prince. "Whoever you think I am, I'm sure we can come to some arrangement. Once I marry the Sultan's daughter—"

In response, Jafar began to cackle. "I don't think I need your arrangement," he said, his voice full of hate.

Aladdin paled as reality sunk in. Jafar knew who he was. It would be the vizier's word against his, and chances were the Sultan was going to believe Jafar. And if that happened, then he could kiss everything, including a future with Jasmine, goodbye.

"You see," Jafar went on, "if I throw you from this balcony, and if you are who you say you are, you'll die a watery death and I'll be free of Prince Ali." He walked over and swung open the balcony doors. The sound of lapping water in the palace moat could be heard far below. "If you survive, it can only be because you have the lamp. In which case, I'll have my answer. So, for the last time, *where is the lamp?*"

Aladdin began to shake his head, reality crashing down. There was no way he could possibly get out of this. This wasn't like stealing an apple from a vendor and talking his way out of paying. This was the kingdom's vizier. Jafar wanted him gone.

And he had the power, and the guards, to make that happen. "Listen to me, I don't know who you think I am—" Aladdin's protest fell short.

As he held up a finger, a cruel smile spread over Jafar's face. "Goodbye . . . Aladdin." Then, turning to his guards, he signaled to two of the bigger ones. The men stepped forward, and with another nod from Jafar, they picked up the chair—with Aladdin still tied to it—and threw it off the side of the balcony.

Aladdin fell. Faster and faster he dropped down, the wind whipping at his hair, howling in his ears. In the fleeting moment he had, he couldn't help thinking that the last time he had felt the wind, it had been flying with Jasmine. This time was much, *much* different.

Desperately, he tugged at the ropes holding him in the chair. But it was no use. They were tight, and he was falling too fast.

With a splash, he hit the murky water of the moat. There was a brief flash of light and he was able to take one big gasp of air before the world went wavy. Swiftly, he began to sink, the weight of the chair making him sink faster. He frantically tried to make out anything in the dark abyss. But all he could see was blackness. His lungs already felt like they were going to explode. He should have just told Jafar the truth. Found the lamp and handed it over. Just like he should have told Jasmine who he really was. But now it was too late. There was no way he was going to survive.

And then, like a mirage in the desert, he saw something. The lamp! It was floating down after him. *Abu!* Aladdin thought, as a wave of hope rushed over him. Abu must have gotten away and found the lamp. He had a chance now. A slim one, but a slim one was better than nothing at all.

A moment later, the legs of the chair hit the sandy bottom of the moat and it sank to its side, with Aladdin still attached. Desperately, he watched as the lamp slowly drifted down, down, down, until it, too, hit the bottom a few feet from where he lay.

Aladdin didn't waste a moment. With all his remaining strength, he began to roll himself— and the chair—over. One painful roll at a time he moved until, finally, he was right next to the lamp. His fingers were mere inches from it. He strained to reach out and touch his fingertips to the brass. But the effort took the last of his breath, and he felt his lungs begin to give in, his eyes begin to close. He wasn't going to make it. After all he had done to try and win over Jasmine, after all he had been through on the streets, he was going to die at the bottom of a moat, and no one would ever know.

No!

The voice inside Aladdin's head was loud, and it shocked his eyes back open. He inched just a bit closer and then, just as his eyes closed again, he rubbed the lamp. The world went dark.

Unconscious, Aladdin didn't see the Genie suddenly appear. Nor did he see him hesitate, confused to find himself underwater. But it took only a moment for the powerful being to figure out where he was, and when he spotted Aladdin, panic filled his face. The Genie rushed forward, shaking him. But Aladdin didn't respond. "Kid, I can't help you with this one," he said desperately. "You gotta wish!" He poked at Aladdin's floating body. Still nothing. "Come on! Say the words. 'I, Aladdin, being of sound mind and body, do wish—'" He stopped. It was no use. Reaching out, he squished Aladdin's lips together, forming the words with his own fingers. He leaned closer, hoping for something. But all he got was silence.

In that moment, the Genie did something that, if Aladdin had been awake, would have surprised and touched him. He pretended he *did* hear something. Something specific. Still moving Aladdin's lips, he spoke for him. "My second wish is to be saved from certain doom at said time of happening. . . ." The wish made, Genie grabbed Aladdin and rocketed toward the surface.

Chapter

Seventeen

"Come on, kid! Kid, wake up! You in there?"

Aladdin heard the Genie's voice, but it sounded foggy and far away. His head was pounding, and his lungs felt heavy. He didn't want to move, but a sudden gagging feeling sent his eyes flying open and his body forward as he coughed up a mouthful of water. As he coughed and gagged, struggling to catch his breath, he remembered everything that had happened: Jafar having him thrown over the balcony, the despair, and then the surge of hope as he saw the lamp. The last thing he remembered was seeing the Genie flash in front of him.

And now he was alive and safe, back in his chambers.

The Genie had saved him.

Despite his rules about favors and friendship, the Genie had somehow, for some reason, managed to pull him out of the water and save his life.

There was nothing he could say or do to ever repay him. But he could try.

Gesturing to him, Aladdin struggled to speak. But his throat was raw and the effort painful. He crooked a finger, trying to get the Genie to lean in still closer. Rolling his eyes, but doing as asked, the Genie bent down. "Thanks, Genie," Aladdin whispered.

To his surprise, the Genie looked embarrassed. "Hey, no problem," he said, trying to brush it off. "I was in the area . . ."

Aladdin shook his head. "I thought you said no favors."

"Well, *technically*, it wasn't—" the Genie countered.

"Thought you said no friends," Aladdin said, getting enough life back in him to enjoy teasing the Genie a bit.

"It actually cost you a wish," the Genie said, trying to gain back the upper hand. But it didn't matter. They both knew what he had done—and what it meant.

"Whatever it cost, thanks. You saved my life." Before the Genie could stop him, Aladdin reached out and gave him a giant hug. Then he pulled back.

While he would have rather stayed in the chambers recovering for a few days—or even weeks, if he was honest—Aladdin knew he couldn't. Genie helped him to a sitting position, offering his arm for support. Aladdin's vision swam as blood flowed back into his brain. When the room had stopped spinning, he spoke again. "We have to stop Jafar."

"Not going to be easy, kid," the Genie said. "He's got everyone under his spell."

Nodding, Aladdin rose and made his way toward the door, each step growing faster. He couldn't waste a minute. Who knew what lies Jafar was telling the Sultan—or worse yet, Jasmine. He had to find them and get his story out. Before the damage was done.

Unfortunately, Jasmine was hearing the whole story—or at least Jafar's version—even as Aladdin and Genie frantically made their way toward the Great Hall. She stood at the end of the Great Hall, listening as her father and Jafar approached.

"And I overheard Prince Ali talking to his advisor about returning with an army to conquer Agrabah—" Jafar said.

"What?" the Sultan cried in disbelief. Jasmine saw the disappointment beginning to cross her father's face. She knew that he had begun to think quite highly of the prince. And now his most valued advisor was spewing a hateful story that made Ali look like a monster.

Jafar nodded. "Now it appears he's fled in the night. I have warned you, my sultan. Agrabah is vulnerable. You must sign off on the invasion before . . ."

Jasmine had heard enough. There was no way any of this was true. And she had only an hour ago left the prince. He hadn't fled. He was probably sleeping in his chambers! "Jafar cannot be trusted!" she said, her face stony as she stared at the vizier.

As if on cue, the door to the Great Hall swung open, revealing Prince Ali. He was disheveled and appeared to have gone swimming—in his clothes— but he was there. Jasmine began to smile. To her surprise, so did Jafar. But his smile was cold and calculating and made hers fade. She narrowed her eyes, wondering what was going on between the vizier and Prince Ali.

"Your Highness," Prince Ali said, rushing

forward. "Your advisor is not who he says he is." He paused, catching his breath.

Instantly, Aladdin's handsome attendant stepped forward and continued the story. "Tied the boy to a chair," he asserted. "Threw him in the water. You know what? I'm no longer calling you Jafar, I'm calling you *too far*—cause that's where you've gone with this."

"Terrible—" the Sultan said. "Just terrible."

Jasmine turned and looked at her father. He sounded strange. And his eyes suddenly looked cloudy, as though he weren't altogether there. It was as if he were a puppet, saying something but not in control.

The Sultan nodded. "Jafar, your loyalty belongs to me," he said, his voice expressionless. Then he turned to Ali. "You invited yourself into our city and we welcomed you as our guest. But I believe your intentions are deceitful. You are a grave danger to Agrabah and you shall be dealt with as such."

Jasmine opened her mouth to protest but her father lifted a hand. He shook his head. "Jafar has told me of Prince Ali's intention. He's here for my throne. Hakim!" His shout echoed off the walls of the Great Hall, but it was not loud enough to drown out the sound of her own heart pounding frantically in her chest. She couldn't let Hakim take Ali. If he did . . .

Suddenly, Prince Ali stepped forward and snatched the staff Jafar had been holding right out of his hands. As the vizier let out a shout of protest, Jasmine noticed that the eyes of the snake on the staff seemed to be glowing bright red. As soon as the staff was out of Jafar's hands, the eyes went dark. And her father seemed to come back to life.

"What . . . what happened?" he asked.

Jasmine was curious to know herself. She wouldn't have believed it if she hadn't seen it, but somehow, Jafar had been controlling her father.

"He's had you under his spell," Prince Ali explained. He held up the staff. Carefully, as though the snake might come to life and hiss at any moment, Ali handed the staff to the Sultan. "He wants your throne."

Looking down at the staff, the Sultan's eyes narrowed. Then he looked back up at Jafar. The man was slinking toward the exit. "My most *trusted* advisor," the Sultan said, sarcasm lacing his voice. He tossed the staff to the ground and then gestured to Hakim. "Have him locked in the dungeon."

The guards began to move toward Jafar. The vizier looked back and forth between the door and the men. Then he shook his head. "I don't think so," he said. And before anyone could stop him, he pulled an object out of his pocket and held it up. The area in front of him filled with smoke. When it cleared, he was gone.

"Find him," the Sultan ordered the guards. As they filed out of the room, he turned back to Ali. "I must apologize for how you have been treated," he said genuinely. "Your honor and integrity will never again be questioned in Agrabah."

Jasmine glanced at Ali. His cheeks were flushed with embarrassment and he swayed nervously back and forth. For someone who had shown no fear at flying on a carpet or walking the streets of an unknown city, he seemed almost frightened of the kindness and respect her father was now offering. It made him, she thought, flushing herself, even more charming.

The Sultan went on. "A more noble, sincere young man has never graced the chambers of this palace. I would be honored to call you my son . . . if that were something anyone wanted."

As Jasmine's blush grew deeper, she locked eyes

with the prince. She couldn't help noticing that even though he had just been given permission to marry her, he didn't seem entirely happy. In fact, he looked almost . . . pained.

Aladdin *was* in pain. Not physically, although he did feel rather sore from his chair tumble into the moat. But that paled in comparison to the pain he was feeling as the Sultan's words sank in and he realized he was now completely, permanently, unequivocally trapped in the big fat lie that was Prince Ali.

As if his body were being controlled by someone else, he went through the motions of shaking the Sultan's hand and squeezing Jasmine's. But as they both spoke to him, he heard only hollow sounds, the blood pumping through his head drowning out everything else. By the time he managed to extricate himself from their company, he felt exhausted. And by the time he and the Genie got back to his chambers, he was pretty sure he wanted to be sick.

Genie didn't seem all too happy, either. "I can't

believe you didn't tell her!" he said, slapping his own forehead in frustration.

Aladdin raised an eyebrow. Was the Genie serious? Had he not just been in the room? "The Sultan *just* finished saying how honest and noble I am . . ." He didn't bother to finish. The irony was obvious to both of them.

"Well," the Genie said with a shrug, "you're not getting any *more* honest and noble stringing this out."

Aladdin took a deep breath. The Genie was right. It wasn't going to get any easier to pull himself out of his lie. The lies were going to pile on top of lies. The sooner he ended the charade, the better. But he wasn't ready to tell her. Not yet, at least.

"Then when?" the Genie asked when Aladdin admitted he was going to wait.

"When the time is right," he answered.

The Genie narrowed his eyes. Aladdin shifted uncomfortably under his gaze. The Genie was no fool. He had lived hundreds of years. He had seen thousands of moments and met hundreds of people. He could tell when someone wasn't being honest. Because, truth be told, Aladdin wasn't just lying to Jasmine and her father, he was lying to himself. About everything. "It's just, they all think I'm—" Aladdin started to say.

"Something you're not," the Genie finished for him. He shook his head, disappointment filling his eyes. "And you're allowing them to continue to think that. Some people call that a lie. I'm starting to think that you have no intention of telling her."

Aladdin opened his mouth to protest. But no words came.

The Genie began to shake his head. "And that whole thing in the desert," he said softly. "The 'I'm going to set you free for my third wish' is a lie, too." He ignored Aladdin's weak protest. Holding up a hand, he stopped him from trying to talk. "Remember when I said there's always that guy? Crazed for money and power . . ." Aladdin nodded. "Here's the problem with that guy. Nothing will ever be enough for somebody who can't ever get enough because, deep down, he feels like *he's* not enough. When I met you, I thought you'd got sent to the cave to get the lamp for that guy. But I'm getting scared that you might be *becoming* that guy."

The Genie's words hit Aladdin like a slap across the face. Was the Genie right? Was he becoming *that* guy? He had never meant to hurt anyone—especially not Jasmine or the Genie. But they didn't know what it was like to be him. What his life had been like. Anger slowly began to bubble up inside Aladdin, replacing the guilty feeling. It wasn't fair of the Genie to judge him. He barely knew him! What right did he have to sit there and pass judgment about Aladdin's behavior when he was a magical being with infinite power? He had probably never known what it was like to love someone he couldn't have or to starve because he couldn't steal food. The anger boiled over and Aladdin lashed out. "You don't get it, Genie. People like me don't get anything *except* by pretending."

"Maybe *you* don't get it," the Genie snapped. "The more you gain by pretending, the less you'll actually have." He paused, hoping to see some recognition in Aladdin's eyes, but Aladdin wouldn't even make eye contact. "You know, in ten thousand years I've never once called a master friend? Broke the rules for you. Saved your life. And for what?" Shaking his head in disappointment, the Genie raised a hand and transformed into a puff of smoke, retreating into his lamp.

"Hey!" Aladdin picked up the lamp and yelled

at it. "I'm not done talking to you!" But the Genie stayed inside, his only response resounding silence. Angrily, Aladdin shoved the lamp into his pocket. He had to get out of there. The chamber rooms felt like they were closing in around him and the air felt thick with the Genie's disappointment. Looking over at Abu and the carpet, he gestured for them to join him. "Come on," he said.

To his surprise, the carpet didn't fly right over. Instead, it turned away. Abu just stood there, looking at him with big, sad eyes. It was clear that neither of them were pleased with his behavior. He narrowed his eyes at Abu. *Traitor,* he thought. Turning his back, he strode out of the room. He didn't need them. He didn't need anyone. He just needed to get out of there. Now.

He had only gotten a few steps when he heard Abu chattering behind him. Not turning to look, he waited until he felt his friend jump on his shoulder. Then he looked at him and gave him a small smile. At least he wasn't completely alone. He would always have Abu. Together, the pair left the palace, heading into Agrabah.

It had only been a few days, but the streets of the city felt like a foreign place to Aladdin. As he walked down an alley, he noticed how grimy it was in comparison to the palace, how the smell of filth filled the air the way the smell of flowers filled the palace gardens. He couldn't return to this life. He just couldn't. Not now that he had tasted freedom from it.

"Who does he think he is?" Aladdin fumed to Abu as he walked. The escape from his chambers was doing little to make him forget his fight with the Genie. "He's supposed to serve me, right?" Stomping along, he didn't notice when an old man emerged from the shadows, hands held out in the hopes of a scrap of something, anything. It wasn't until he bumped right into the beggar that Aladdin even took notice. He quickly brushed him aside. "Watch where you're going!" he said, continuing on without a backward look at the beggar. "I'm the same as I always was . . . on the inside. Right?" He looked at Abu. The monkey didn't squeak or chatter. He just looked down at the ground.

Aladdin gulped. Maybe the Genie *had* been right. Maybe he *had* changed. And if that was true, he knew it wasn't for the better. Aladdin sighed deeply. It looked like he owed his friend a serious apology. And he owed Jasmine the truth.

Chapter
Eighteen

The Genie was angry. He was angrier than he had been in over nine thousand years. There had been that one time when his master had made him separate a puppy from its mother that had really irked him. But that was nothing compared to how angry Aladdin's betrayal made him now. To think, he had believed the kid was different from the hundreds of other people who had rubbed his lamp. He had thought he was kind. He had thought he might help him out.

Well, the joke was on him.

Feeling the familiar sensation of someone rubbing the outside of the lamp, he steeled himself to face Aladdin. But to his surprise, when he was pulled free of the lamp, it wasn't Aladdin's face he found himself looking at.

It was Jafar's.

"Ah, tragedy . . ." Genie said, none too pleased by the turn of events. "Not what I expected."

Jafar, who was dressed as the beggar Aladdin had so callously brushed aside, threw back his hood. An evil smile crossed over his face. Stealing the lamp from Aladdin had been so gloriously simple. And now he was the one in charge. "I think you know how to address me," he said to the Genie.

The Genie let out a sigh. *This* was all too familiar. "Oh, Great One who summons me," he said, unhappily conceding to his usual role, "and Terrible One who commands me . . ."

As Jafar rubbed his hands together greedily, the Genie glanced up toward the palace. Aladdin had frustrated him, but at that moment, he would have done anything to see his friend's face instead of this guy's. At least that way, he knew what to expect. Jafar was an unknown. But from the evil look in his eye and from what the Genie already knew about the vizier, he had a guess that whatever Jafar wanted, it wasn't good.

Morning light streamed through the windows of her chamber, making the gold filigree in her curtains sparkle. A warm wind blew, carrying with it the scent of the garden and the peaceful sound of birdsong. But despite the idyllic moment, Jasmine's brows were furrowed, her thoughts troubled.

Looking over at the princess, Dalia frowned. Jasmine should be over the moon. The Sultan had given her permission to marry Prince Ali. He had practically begged the prince, in fact. And after their magical carpet ride, Jasmine had been a puddle of happiness. So why was she suddenly unhappy? "Are you okay?" Dalia asked. She smiled teasingly. "Is it that whole 'finding the man of your dreams and your life is perfect' thing?"

Jasmine looked over and gave Dalia a small smile. "I know, I should be happy," she admitted. "He's a wonderful man and I should just accept that Baba will never see me as a leader. But I can't settle for that. Do you understand . . . ?" Her voice trailed off.

Dalia shook her head. "No," she said. "But I do love you."

Jasmine sighed. She knew that she was being stubborn and prideful. She knew that complaining to Dalia, who had even less choice and freedom than she did, was somewhat ironic and a bit cruel. And she knew that in the grand scheme of things, it could have been a lot worse. If Prince Ali hadn't shown up, she might have ended up married to Prince Anders and living in Skånland. As it was, she had the chance of marrying for love now—or at least, she *felt* she was starting to love Ali. Suddenly, a thought flew into her mind. A thought that gave her the smallest flicker of hope. She knew Ali cared for her, too. And he *had* said he thought she had what it took to be a wonderful leader. . . . So what if he would be willing to allow her to be more than just his wife? Maybe, just maybe, he would let her help him rule. . . .

With a sense of renewed hope, Jasmine turned to her closet. It was time to get dressed and greet the day. She had a future husband to see and plans to make. And she intended to let nothing get in her way. . . .

And that was when she heard the crash. Glancing at Dalia, who stared back at her with large, frightened eyes, Jasmine threw on an outfit and headed toward the Great Hall.

While Jasmine had been blissfully preparing to greet the day, Jafar had been evilly preparing to take it over—and Agrabah and, quite possibly, the world if he could. Lounging in the Sultan's chair in the Great Hall, he absently moved the magical lamp he had stolen back from Aladdin from one hand to the other. He shifted uncomfortably on the hard seat. First thing he was going to do—after the whole business of becoming sultan—was get a new throne. Something grander; something softer. Growing bored, he stretched out a leg, pushing over a heavy iron vase. It fell to the floor with a resounding crash.

The noise was like an alarm. Instantly, Jafar heard the sound of footsteps outside the door. He smiled. Then he leaned back and waited. A moment later, the door flew open and the Sultan and Hakim burst in. Jasmine, Dalia, and Raja were close behind.

"Jafar!" the Sultan said when he saw his former vizier sitting in his throne. "You should have left Agrabah while you had the chance." Behind him, the rest of his guards appeared, filling up the hall and blocking the exits. But to the Sultan's surprise, Jafar didn't look worried. In fact, he looked downright smug.

"Why leave a city that belongs to me now?" he

asked. He lifted what looked like an old brass lamp up in front of him.

Jasmine's eyes narrowed. Beside her, Raja growled and pressed himself closer to Jasmine.

"It's over for you, Jafar," the Sultan continued, ignoring the lamp and Raja's growls.

Jafar shook his head. "No, it's over for you, old man," he countered. As he spoke, he rose to his feet. He stood looking down at the Sultan. "I've endured your spineless incompetence for long enough now. . . ." Lifting the lamp, he rubbed its side.

Blue smoke began to pour from the spout, filling the Great Hall. Beside Jasmine, Raja stood at attention, hackles raised. Jasmine felt her heart start to pound and she took an unconscious step backward. When the smoke finally cleared, there, hovering in the air beside Jafar, was a genie—a giant blue entity floating in the Great Hall. A giant blue entity who, inconceivably, looked oddly familiar. Jasmine gasped. She had heard stories of the powerful creatures but hadn't believed them. Until now.

"Genie," Jafar sneered. "For my first wish, I wish to be sultan of Agrabah!"

"What?" the Sultan said.

But it was too late. Jafar's wish had been made. And it seemed the Genie had no choice but to make it come true. He lifted his great blue hands, and thunder and lightning filled the air as magic began to transform Jafar into a sultan. At the same time, the palace began to transform, too. The beautiful objects collected by Jasmine's parents became objects of darkness, snakes and scorpions covering the walls and pillars that turned from gold to black. What had been good now became evil. What had been beautiful was now ugly. Jasmine's throat tightened, and tears stung her eyes as she watched the transformation take place.

"Hakim!" the Sultan shouted to the head of his guards.

But the Sultan was no longer sultan. And the guards were no longer his guards. They answered to Jafar. So when he told some of them to marshal an army and prepare to invade Shirabad, they didn't question him. They turned, in perfect sync, and began to head out of the Great Hall.

Jasmine watched them, anger replacing her fear and sadness. "You can't do that!" she shouted, stepping forward. Turning, Jafar looked at her as if just noticing her. He raised an eyebrow as she went on. "That is where my mother . . . They are our *allies*!"

"I think we've all heard enough from you, Princess," he said when she had finished. "It's time you start doing what should have been done all along—stay silent." He turned to the remaining guards. "Remove her," he ordered.

Strong hands locked around Jasmine's arms and she struggled angrily in their grasp. She thought back to the market when she had also been taken captive. As she was dragged from the hall, she looked back over her shoulder at her father. Sadness covered his face. Behind him, Jafar stood, his new dark cape flowing over his shoulders, his face full of victory.

I won't let him win, Jasmine thought as the doors slammed shut behind her, blocking her father from view. *Jafar wants me silent? Well, he is in for a surprise. As long as I'm breathing, I'm going to fight. I won't stay silent. Not now. Not ever again.*

Letting out a shout, she pulled free from the surprised guards—who had thought she would go easily—and sprinted back toward the Great Hall. Bursting through the doors, she raced down the long room, coming to a stop in front of the men. Instantly, her arms were locked in the hands of new guards. "Hakim!" she cried.

"Take her away!" Jafar shouted angrily. "Tell them, Hakim."

But Hakim hesitated. Seeing her chance, Jasmine looked at her old friend, imploring him. "You were just a boy when your father came here to work the grounds. But you've risen up to become our most trusted soldier." She paused, hoping to see a flicker of something in Hakim's eyes. But the man remained still, his expression blank. She pressed on. She *needed* to get through to him. "I know you to be both loyal and just. But now you have to choose. Duty isn't always honor. Our greatest challenge isn't speaking out against our enemies, it's defying those whose approval we seek most." She pointed at Jafar. "He is not worthy of your admiration nor your sacrifice." Jasmine grew silent, her words echoing off the walls of the Great Hall. She could feel her father's eyes on her, as well as Jafar's. But she ignored them both, instead looking to see if she had gotten through to Hakim. She knew what it was to so desperately want to do what others asked, at the cost of her own happiness. She had to believe that Hakim had heard the truth in her pleas. If not, she was lost.

"Silence, you silly girl," Jafar said, letting out a laugh as Hakim remained still. "I seek glory for the kingdom of Agrabah."

Jasmine shook her head. How foolish and silly did he think she was? He did not seek glory for anyone but himself. And he would win it no matter the cost. The people of Agrabah would suffer. Turning from Jafar, she once again focused on Hakim. Jafar was evil, through and through. There was no chance he would bend. But Hakim was like family. She could get through to him. She *had* to get through to him. She pointed to the guards, who awaited their orders. "Hakim, these men will follow where you lead, but it's up to you. Will you stand silent while Jafar destroys our beloved kingdom, or will you do what is right . . . and stand *with* the people of Agrabah?"

Jasmine held her breath as Hakim looked back and forth between her and Jafar. She could see the hesitation in his eyes—he was torn between loyalty and duty. But then he took a step closer to Jasmine. He bowed ever so slightly. Behind him, the guards did the same. "I will follow you, my princess.

Forgive me, my sultan." He looked to his men. "Guards! Arrest the vizier."

As the guards stepped forward to take Jafar captive, Jasmine smiled. She knew it wasn't the perfect time; in fact it was a rather terrible situation, but she had done it. She had made Hakim hear her. She had not stood by, speechless and powerless. She had been a leader.

Yet the smile faded on her lips as she looked over at Jafar. The air around him seemed to have grown darker and his face was full of fury. She may have won over Hakim and the guards, but she had just made a very powerful enemy.

As the guards moved to grab Jafar, he stepped back, evading their grasp. Rage filled his face and made his dark features even darker. "So, this is how it will be," he sneered. "Not even the title of sultan will wake the herd from their sleep." He shook his head. "I should have known." Lifting the lamp high into the air, he rubbed its side. In a puff of smoke, the Genie appeared, his face full of anguish. "If you won't bow before a sultan," he said in a rage, "you'll cower before a sorcerer!" He looked at the Genie. "I wish to become the most powerful sorcerer there is!"

Instantly, there was an explosion of magic. Colors lit up the room, illuminating the walls in a riot of reds and yellows and greens, like a magical fireworks display. Thunder boomed and echoed, shaking the room. When the magic finally cleared, Jafar emerged from the smoke. His cape, now a deep and violent red streaked with gold, swirled out behind him, the hat on his head dark and pulled tight, making his eyebrows arch even more severely. A snake slithered out from behind him, twirling around his feet and then up, until it, too, transformed—into a giant new staff. The staff, the same dark red and gold as Jafar's robes, was more ornate than the small one he'd used to yield. It pulsed with untapped power—and untapped evil.

Chapter

Nineteen

idden in the shadows of the Great Hall, Aladdin swelled with pride as he saw Jasmine stand up for Agrabah. He watched as she used the power of her beliefs with eloquence to sway Hakim to her cause, and then he watched as Jafar grew furious.

He had been in the market when he'd seen the first signs of trouble. Blue smoke billowing from the windows of the Great Hall had him reaching for his pocket. Finding it empty, he had hit himself on the head. How foolish could he have been? The beggar? The random bump in the middle of an otherwise empty alley? It could only have been Jafar. The vizier had managed to steal the lamp and, from the looks of it, he was putting the Genie to work.

Aladdin had raced back to the palace and arrived in the Great Hall just in time to see Jafar make his first wish. Now he waited to see what would happen next.

He didn't have to wait long.

Unaware of Aladdin, Jafar let out an evil cackle. Reveling in his strength, he looked around the room, and his gaze stopped on Hakim. "I had such big plans for you," he said to the guard. "But now you're no use to me. Perhaps your men could follow you to the dungeon."

The guards began to move toward Hakim, clearly under Jafar's spell. Using their footsteps as cover, Aladdin took a few steps forward, his arm outstretched, his fingers nearly touching the lamp . . .

BANG!

Jafar slammed his staff down on the ground, mere inches from Aladdin's fingers. Aladdin fell to his knees, looking up into Jafar's sinister eyes. The sorcerer looked back down at him and sneered. "If it isn't our Prince Ali."

"Ali!" Aladdin heard Jasmine's hopeful shout, but he didn't turn around. He needed to stay focused and be ready for whatever Jafar threw at him next.

The sorcerer banged his staff on the ground

once more, sending another violent quake through the room. "Or should I say, *Aladdin*," he said. He waved the staff over Aladdin, and the air filled with smoke.

Aladdin felt a strange sensation, as if he were being tugged at by a million unseen fingers. When the smoke cleared, he looked down—and then he groaned. Gone were the fancy clothes of Prince Ali. Once more, he was clad in the ragged apparel of a street rat. Slowly, he lifted his head. His eyes met Jasmine's and he shrugged weakly. *Guess she knows the truth now,* he thought sadly.

"He's an imposter," Jafar said, clearly taking pleasure in revealing Aladdin's secret. "A thief, and not even a very good one." He raised the lamp. "Even with the lamp, you couldn't wish yourself worthy of a princess. You're insignificant . . . an irritation I no longer need to tolerate once I ensure your agonizing death by"—he raised the staff in the air, the snake's eyes glowing more and more crimson as a surge of magical power flowed through it—"banishing you to the ends of the earth!"

The last thing Aladdin heard before the world around him disappeared was the frightened gasps of Jasmine and her father. As he desperately reached out a hand, he saw Abu rush forward. Aladdin wanted to smile. Even now, when things couldn't possibly get worse, his friend wasn't going to leave his side. Just as the monkey reached him, the world went white and then everything—and everyone—vanished.

Jasmine stared at the spot where, only moments before, Ali—or rather, Aladdin—had stood. Now nothing remained. He had simply vanished into thin air.

And she had no idea where he had gone—or what to think.

Aladdin had lied. Not just a single lie, either. He had lied to her over and over again. He had lied straight to her face even when she had called him out for being the young man from the marketplace. And he had made her feel so silly for thinking he wasn't a prince. She should've been furious with him. But somehow, she wasn't. In fact, if anything, she was simply scared. Scared that he was gone and would never come back. Scared that maybe she was the one lying to herself, because if she thought about it, really thought about it, she had suspected all along something was off. It had just been easier to believe Aladdin was the prince he pretended to be.

Sighing, she realized that her fear of never seeing Aladdin again was becoming more likely. Jafar's mood had only worsened in the past few minutes. She watched apprehensively as he paced in front of the throne, his knuckles white as he clenched his staff. Stopping, he stared down at those still remaining in the Great Hall. "Now, I could simply kill you all," he began. "But that would be inadequate repayment for years of humiliation and neglect." Finally, he stopped and stared at the Sultan. "What you need is to suffer."

Jasmine let out a cry as Jafar brought down his staff, sending a magical burst of pain through the Sultan that brought the older man to his knees. He lay on the floor, his hands clutching at his chest while Jasmine looked around, desperate to do something. Jafar seemed to be enjoying every minute of her father's agony.

"Would watching me rule your kingdom be enough?" Jafar went on. His eyes landed on Jasmine. She felt them bore into her, like icy daggers. "Oh, you think this is pain, Princess?" He shook his head. Once more, he addressed the Sultan. "No . . . I think the most suitable punishment would be to make you watch while I take what you value most . . . and marry your daughter."

"No!" The shout tore out of Jasmine before she could even think to stop it. Marry Jafar? She would rather die. The thought alone made her stomach turn. If she had thought marrying a prince would render her powerless, she could only imagine what being married to Jafar would mean. A life of misery, silence, not being heard. Her chance of having any say in the future and happiness of her people would be gone. She shook her head. *No,* she thought again. She could never marry that man.

Her father seemed to agree. Struggling to his feet, he took a step closer to Jafar. "She'll never marry you—" he said shakily.

Jafar shrugged. "Then I'll kill her precious baba," he said, as if the act of murdering the Sultan would be as easy and painless to him as swatting a fly. Raising his staff, he once again began to flood the older man with bolts of pain. The Sultan writhed, looking like a marionette dancing on its strings. His face grew paler and paler as the pain became unbearable.

Tears began to fall from Jasmine's eyes at the sight of her father's torment. Jafar was killing him. She wiped angrily at her cheeks. She knew there was only one way to stop him and save her father. Stepping forward, she raised a hand. "Stop," she cried. "I will do as you ask."

"Will you marry me?" Jafar asked.

Jasmine nodded. "Yes, just make it stop."

Instantly, the Sultan stopped thrashing. He fell to the ground, drained.

"Very good," Jafar said, turning to leave. "Glad we got that out of the way. See you at the wedding." He nodded to the guards, who now were quaking in their boots and seemed to be very much in his control—with or without magic. Jafar ordered them to make sure Jasmine behaved. Then he left.

As soon as he was gone, Jasmine rushed over to her father. Crouching beside him, she pulled his head into her lap. As she gently stroked his hair, she whispered, "Don't worry." But she knew her words sounded hollow.

Jasmine did everything in her power to delay the wedding. She tried on ten different dresses to waste time. She had Dalia take her shoes to the cobbler in the market even though they didn't need mending. She took Raja outside for a walk and then reorganized her maps by date of creation. But finally, it was clear she could delay it no longer.

She was going to marry Jafar.

With heavy footsteps and an even heavier heart, she made her way toward one of the larger palace balconies. Jafar was already there, leering at an imam he had summoned to perform the ceremony. The poor imam looked terrified, and Jasmine could only imagine what Jafar had told him the consequence would be if he did *not* agree to marry them. The man's shaking hands held the book with the vows. To the side, held back by two guards, was the Sultan. He looked like he had aged twenty years in the past two hours. The bags under his eyes were deep and his shoulders stooped. As he met Jasmine's gaze, she saw that he was crying. Her own eyes welled up in response. This was not how she had expected her wedding to go. She had pictured flowers and music and her friends and loved ones around her. She had imagined hushed gasps as she walked in wearing the purple gown her mother had worn at her own wedding, every inch covered with opalescent beading. Turquoise covering the neckline and plunging down the back, a nod to the brightness and beauty of Agrabah's sea. And most important, she had expected the groom greeting her to make her heart race with happiness, not make her stomach lurch with disgust.

Finally, she arrived in front of Jafar. He stepped forward, taking his place next to Jasmine. Then he looked up at the imam expectantly.

The imam opened and closed his mouth like a dying fish. But no words came out and his hands just began to shake more.

"Stop shaking and do your job," Jafar hissed.

The imam nodded nervously. "Jafar," he began, "in all honesty and sincerity, do you take Princess Jasmine to be your wife?"

"I pledge," Jafar began, "in honesty and sincerity to look after you, Princess."

Jasmine looked over at him, not bothering to hide the revulsion that coursed through her. Look after her? They both knew what he really meant. He would have been sincerer if he had said, *I plan to keep you prisoner for the rest of your life, Princess.*

"Princess Jasmine?" the imam said, turning his frightened gaze toward her now.

Jasmine swallowed back the bile that rose in her throat. She looked over at her father. She had to do this. If she didn't, Jafar would kill him. "I . . . I . . ." she stammered, the words sticking in her throat. Jafar stared, eyeing her as though he were a cat and she were the mouse. Desperately, Jasmine looked around the balcony, hoping that by some miracle she could find a way out of this.

And then she saw Dalia. Her handmaiden mouthed the word, *Look!* and nodded her head over her shoulder. Following her gaze, Jasmine nearly let out a shout of happiness. There, hurtling toward the palace on the carpet, was Aladdin. He was alive!

Before Jafar could turn to see what she was looking at, Jasmine once more began to speak. "I . . ." she said, lifting her hand ever so slightly, "do . . ." Her fingers stretched out. And then, just as she added the word "not!" she grabbed hold of the lamp from Jafar's waist belt.

At the very same moment, Aladdin swooped over them and held out his hand. "Jump!" he shouted to Jasmine.

Without hesitation, Jasmine leapt onto the carpet. They soared away, hearing Jafar's angry shouts of protest. Turning, Jasmine saw a burst of magic pour from the staff in his hands, and Iago the pesky parrot transformed into a huge, menacing phoenix.

Lifting into the air, Iago let out an angry squawk and took off after them. Jasmine grabbed Aladdin's arm as the carpet picked up speed and headed away from the palace toward the center of Agrabah. They had to get away. Luckily, Jasmine happened to know Aladdin was quite good at evading capture. She just had to hope that his skill extended to the skies.

Chapter
Twenty

As the carpet flew them toward the market of
Agrabah, Aladdin kept his eyes straight
ahead. He could hear Jasmine's frightened breathing and felt her hand clutching his arm.
He knew he had to say something, but where could
he even begin? Should he tell her he had done all
this for her? Should he tell her that when Jafar suddenly banished him to the ends of the earth, the
only thing that kept him warm in those moments
stuck in a frozen wasteland he found himself in
was the thought of her? Should he tell her that
when the carpet had appeared, he had nearly wept
with joy at being found because he just wanted to
get back to her? Should he tell her that all he could
think of on the long carpet ride back was the one
they had shared together? Should he tell her that
as they flew toward the city he knew he loved her?
Would that be enough? Could it ever be enough?

"Why did you lie to me?"

Jasmine's voice broke into his thoughts, sending a fresh wave of guilt through him. He raised his eyes, meeting her gaze. She was staring at him. But to his astonishment, the anger he had thought he would find there was missing. Instead, she was gazing at him with a combination of sadness and curiosity. He sighed. He could make up even more lies, but what was the point? If there was ever a time to be honest, it was now. "Who'd want a street rat?" he asked softly.

"Is that what you think you are?" Jasmine responded, sounding surprised by the question.

Aladdin opened his mouth to answer, but a loud screeching cry from close behind made him turn instead. His eyes grew wide with fear as he saw Iago—still in the form of a terrifying phoenix—closing in on them. With a giant beat of his long wings, the bird caught up to them. Opening his beak, Iago snapped at the carpet, nearly getting hold of Aladdin. As Abu leapt up from his spot on the carpet to try and save his friend, Jasmine screamed and the lamp fell from her grasp. It dropped toward the market.

Acting quickly, Aladdin steered the carpet away from the phoenix and then urged it to swoop down. "Abu!" Aladdin cried to his friend. "Get the lamp!" With a nod, the monkey edged closer to the side of the carpet. Just as the carpet flew over a stall full of lamps, Abu jumped. Frantically, he began to search through the myriad of lamps. He chattered in frustration as he picked up one after another, all of which looked exactly like the Genie's.

Meanwhile, Aladdin and Jasmine led the phoenix on a chase through the market. Aladdin kept one eye on Abu, waiting for a signal from the monkey. The carpet ducked and weaved around stalls of fruits and vegetables, around vendors selling candles and hawking jewels. But no matter how well he maneuvered, Iago the phoenix stayed just a beat behind.

Finally, they heard Abu let out a triumphant shout. Turning the carpet back toward the stall full of lamps, Aladdin brought them right over it. Just as they flew by, Abu threw the lamp up into the air. Aladdin deftly caught it and then, before the phoenix could get any closer, they took off again, heading straight into a tunnel off the side of the market.

"Where are we going?" Jasmine shouted over the wind and the angry cries of the phoenix.

"Trust me!" Aladdin shouted back.

Jasmine raised an eyebrow. "You say that a lot!" she countered. But she nodded and tightened her grip on the carpet as they flew into the darkness.

The tunnel stretched on for miles, a hidden passageway that Aladdin had used to his benefit on more than one occasion when he had been running from guards or angry vendors. He knew that he just had to be patient and his plan would work. But as the phoenix followed them into the tunnel, its cries bouncing off the dark and damp walls, Aladdin swallowed nervously. He had never escaped from an angry magical creature in these tunnels.

Then, up ahead, Aladdin saw something that gave him hope. The walls of the tunnel were growing narrower. He urged the carpet for one more burst of speed, and they flew on. Behind them, unaware of what was happening, came the phoenix. His mouth opened, his neck stretched out, and just when it seemed he was going to catch them, the bird's wings smacked into the tight walls. With a shriek, the phoenix crashed to the ground, erupting in a blaze.

Aladdin let out a triumphant shout, and a

moment later, he turned the carpet down another short tunnel. They burst back out into the bright sunshine. Holding up the lamp, he began to rub it. But then he stopped. There was something he needed to say to Jasmine—and it couldn't wait. "I'm sorry, I—"

She didn't let him finish. "Aladdin! Just rub the lamp!"

He nodded. She had a point. Maybe now wasn't a good time for apologies. Holding up the lamp, he once more began to rub its side. Nothing happened. He rubbed it again. Still nothing happened. Slowly, he lifted his head and looked at Jasmine. "It's the wrong one!" he cried.

At that very moment, the phoenix rose from the ashes, reborn. Letting out an angry cry that echoed throughout the market, it took off after Aladdin and Jasmine. Once more, the carpet began to weave in and around the market as both Jasmine and Aladdin searched in blind panic for Abu—and the correct lamp.

Aladdin's heart raced as his eyes scanned the ground. Then, realizing he hadn't heard the phoenix's cries for a moment, he turned and saw that the bird had stopped chasing them. He scanned the colorful streets and spotted its fiery feathers flying in the opposite direction. Squinting his eyes, he saw it was chasing something else now—Abu! The little monkey was running as fast as he could along the market's numerous rooftops. But he was weighed down by a lamp—*the* lamp— and the phoenix was gaining quickly.

"Abu!" Aladdin shouted. He frantically looked around. He needed to save his friend. But how? Then his eyes brightened. Hadn't he just called himself a street rat? Well, what were street rats good at if not using the streets—and roofs—to their benefit? "Carpet, get me up there, now!" he cried, pointing.

With a wave of its tassels, the carpet headed toward the nearest roof. It paused long enough to let Aladdin leap off. Somersaulting head over heels, Aladdin landed and took off after his friend. His legs burned as he flung himself from one building to the next until, finally, he was mere feet away from Abu. Reaching out, he grabbed the monkey and the lamp and, taking a deep breath, flung himself off the roof . . . and onto the carpet next to Jasmine.

But he wasn't quick enough. Just as he landed on the carpet, the phoenix reached out and snatched the lamp right out of Aladdin's hand. With a triumphant cry, the bird turned and began to fly back toward the palace.

Jasmine gasped. Aladdin watched desperately as Iago flew farther and farther away—the only hope for salvation grasped in his pointy beak. But just as their hopes dimmed almost completely, the bird let out a startled cry and transformed back into his parrot form. Aladdin watched, dumbfounded, as Iago, weighed down by the lamp, began to fall toward the ground.

While he had no idea why Iago was no longer a terrifying phoenix, Aladdin didn't care. It was a chance. And that was just what they needed. Aladdin steered the carpet over to where Iago had fallen, and Abu leapt off the carpet and tackled the parrot. As the animals screeched and cawed, they fought over the lamp. Finally, Abu snatched it back and turned to find Aladdin and Jasmine waiting. Then, with Iago unable to do anything to stop them, they sailed up into the air, disappearing through an open window of one of the houses that lined the market.

In the palace, Jafar's rage was intensifying. He was tired of the foolish—and frankly, ridiculous—attempts by the Sultan to stop him. The older man had tried to tackle him only moments before, forcing Jafar to lose his concentration for a moment. But the moment had been costly. He had heard his phoenix's cries and then the parrot squawks of Iago and known instantly that his lapse in concentration had cost him the lamp—for now. But he would get it back. He'd had enough of Aladdin ruining his plans and making his life difficult. It was about time he put an end to that street rat once and for all. Ignoring the Sultan, who now lay on the ground, unconscious, he lifted his sorcerer's staff into the air. Dark clouds began to form above his head and then swirled outward, darkening the sky around the palace and then all of Agrabah. As lightning began to strike, he transformed the parrot into a phoenix once more, and it let out a loud squawk. The bird would keep chasing Aladdin until he caught him. And if the phoenix didn't get him, the storm would.

Walking to the balcony, Jafar looked out and watched the dark clouds grow thicker and more menacing. He smiled. It was only a matter of time now. Soon he would have his lamp back—and then he would destroy Aladdin, the Sultan, his precious princess . . . and everyone else who stood in his way.

Thunder crashed and lightning tore through the sky. Once again being chased by the phoenix, Aladdin and Jasmine clung to the carpet, trying to evade both the bird and the newly forming storm. But the lightning was coming faster and faster. The sky had grown so dark it was hard to see. And then, suddenly, a bolt flew down from the clouds and struck the carpet.

As Jasmine let out a frightened scream, Aladdin found himself flung off the carpet. He began to fall, one hand holding the lamp, the other outstretched toward the carpet. Hearing the unmistakable beating of wings, he looked over and saw the phoenix close behind. The bird snatched the lamp out of

Aladdin's hand with his beak. A moment later, Jasmine steered the carpet under Aladdin, swiftly catching him. His eyes never left the phoenix as it headed toward the palace.

"We have to go back," Jasmine said, following his gaze. They both knew Jafar couldn't get his hands on that lamp again.

Aladdin shook his head sadly. "If we go back, he'll kill us."

"He'll never stop," Jasmine said. "First a sultan, now a sorcerer . . ." Her voice trailed off as they both imagined the next horror.

"And pretty soon, just being a man won't be enough," Aladdin said. The Genie's fiery words and anger flashed in front of him. He truly understood what the Genie had been trying to tell him—about power never being enough. He couldn't let Jafar continue. He had to stop him. Not only for the kingdom, but for the Genie. He had to show his friend that he wasn't that guy. He might just be a street rat, but he knew the difference between right and wrong. "Carpet," he said, his voice growing strong with renewed determination, "can you get us back over the wall?"

The carpet, its fabric unraveling from the lightning strike, bravely nodded. Turning toward the palace and the dark clouds engulfing it, the group headed toward Jafar—and whatever fate lay in store.

Chapter

Twenty-One

As they flew closer and closer to the palace, the carpet continued to unravel. Clutching what was left of their magical ride, Jasmine and Aladdin held their breath, hoping the carpet would hold out long enough to get them safely into the palace. Aladdin kept his gaze straight ahead, but his mind was whirling. He knew Jafar would stop at nothing to ruin him, and that meant hurting those he cared about, including Jasmine. But he also knew there was no turning back now.

With one last gasp of effort, the carpet hurtled them onto the palace balcony. They tumbled forward, landing in a heap. Beneath them, the carpet had come completely undone. Aladdin checked to make sure that Jasmine and Abu were all right. Then he turned, and his gaze landed on the frightened faces of the Sultan and Dalia and the irate face of Jafar. Finally, he spotted the Genie. Misery was written across his face, and yet he still looked every inch the powerful being that he was. No matter what Jafar did to those around him, he couldn't take that away from the Genie.

Suddenly, Aladdin had an idea. It would mean feeding into Jafar's need for power. But it might just work. . . . And it was something, which right now was a whole lot better than no plan at all.

Jafar locked eyes on him. "You should have left Agrabah when you had the chance," he said coldly. "Why did you come back?" As he spoke, his raised his hands in the air. Both the Sultan and Dalia lifted off the ground, hovering powerlessly several feet above the cold stone of the balcony.

Aladdin's hands clenched as he pushed himself to his feet. "I came back to save you," he said.

Jafar raised an eyebrow. "You came back to *save* me? Touching. For a street thief, you think very highly of yourself. Have you forgotten I have the lamp?" As if to prove his point, the sorcerer lifted the lamp and waved it in front of Aladdin.

"You can't find what you're looking for in that lamp," Aladdin said, his eyes resting on the brass object. "I tried and failed . . ." he added truthfully. "And so will you." He had tried so desperately to be worthy of Jasmine and another life that he'd become a person he wasn't proud of, pushing away those he loved, including her. Genie had been right all along—wishes did not a prince make.

Jafar looked unimpressed by Aladdin's threat. "You think so?" he asked. Then he shook his head. "I don't think I'm going to fail. I can destroy cities, I can destroy kingdoms—and I can destroy you." Once more, he raised his hands. As Aladdin watched, Jasmine lifted into the air, joining her father and handmaiden. Then, suddenly, Aladdin felt his own legs go out from underneath him as he, too, was lifted skyward. He struggled against the magic that began to pull him toward Jafar, but to no avail. The man's power as a sorcerer was too great. All he could do was let himself be carried across the balcony. When he was right in front of Jafar, the magic dropped him to the ground. He found himself on his knees. Satisfied by Aladdin's position, Jafar went on. "I don't think I need you, and I don't think I'll fail."

The magic that had brought him to Jafar was now sending bursts of pain throughout Aladdin. Struggling not to collapse, he looked up at Jafar. "Who made you a sultan?" he asked. "Who made you a sorcerer?" His gaze traveled to the Genie.

His friend looked miserable, knowing that he'd had no choice but to do what was asked, no matter the outcome.

Following his gaze, Jafar let out a nasty laugh. "He serves *me*," he said with a sneer.

Aladdin shrugged. "For now . . ." he said. "But you'll never have more power than the Genie. You can't win this game, Jafar. You're still only a man, after all, and you're still only the second most powerful man in the room." He stopped, waiting to see what effect his words would have on Jafar.

He didn't have to wait long. Just as Aladdin suspected, the idea of being just a man when there was a more powerful option was too much for Jafar to take. He was driven by an insatiable need for more. He wouldn't stand for being second best. Not after doing so for years, as he believed he had.

Looking over at the Genie, Aladdin saw him mouth, *What are you doing?* But Aladdin just shook his head. The Genie would find out soon enough.

"Only a man . . ." Jafar repeated. "I think we can do better than that! Genie," he said, turning and addressing him, "for my final wish, I wish to be the most powerful being in the universe. More powerful than you!"

Aladdin held his breath. Would the Genie get it? Would he see what Aladdin was trying to do? He watched as Genie stood there, processing the wish. And then, a light came into his eyes. Aladdin bit back a shout of happiness.

"The 'most powerful,'" Genie repeated. He bit his lip and looked serious. "Lot of gray area there."

"Do it!" Jafar screamed.

Genie shrugged. "Most powerful being in the world, coming right up." He lifted his hands, and blue smoke began to fill the air around Jafar, covering him in a blanket of blue. The sky above the palace grew darker and then, with a burst of magic more powerful than any of them had yet seen, Jafar's wish came true. He began to grow, stretching into an enormous genie. When the magic faded and the smoke cleared, Jafar towered over them, each wrist wrapped with the golden bands of a genie, his skin now a demonic red.

Stretching out his arms, Jafar let out a booming cry. "I can feel it!" he said, his voice shaking the balcony. "The power of the cosmos coursing through my veins. I am unstoppable!" He raised his hands to conjure up something to demonstrate his powers.

But nothing happened.

He tried again.

Still nothing.

Jafar turned his furious gaze upon Aladdin. "What have you done?" he snarled.

Aladdin shrugged. "I didn't do anything, Jafar," he said, not bothering to keep the pleasure out of his voice. "This was *your* wish, not mine. A genie might have phenomenal cosmic powers . . ." He didn't finish, but instead looked over to the Genie, who happily did so for him.

"But an itty-bitty living space," he said with a smile. "You see, a genie without a master goes in the lamp." He sent Aladdin a proud smile. "Shoulda listened to the kid."

"No! No!" Jafar began to beg as he realized what was about to happen. "I promise I'll be good . . ."

But the Genie ignored him, instead making a lamp appear in the air. Similar to his own, but smaller and less comfortable-looking, it would be Jafar's new home. As Jafar continued to scream and beg, red smoke poured from the spout, reaching out and grabbing hold of him. In moments, Jafar and his beloved parrot were sucked into the lamp. With a puff of smoke, they disappeared.

As Jafar's power completely faded, the skies above the palace began to clear. Black clouds dissipated, replaced by thin white ones. The birds that had stopped singing, thinking it was night, began to warble with glee. Lifting his hand, the Genie lowered Jasmine, the Sultan, and Dalia to the ground. Then he held up Jafar's lamp, bouncing it from one hand to the other as he made it change sizes, knowing full well that, inside, Jafar was feeling pretty cramped. Finally, he pulled back his arm and magically flung the lamp out over the city of Agrabah and into the desert beyond. "A couple thousand years in the Cave of Wonders should cool you off a bit," he said.

Hearing a sad chirp, Genie looked down, surprised. He wouldn't have thought anyone would be bothered by getting rid of Jafar for a good long time. But it wasn't that. At his feet, the Genie saw Abu holding what was left of the carpet in his hands. He looked up at the Genie with desperate eyes. "Ooh, that's a bit of a mess there, Abu. Let me take care of that for you." He waved his hand, and in moments, the carpet was once again whole. The carpet did a little dance, flying up and down happily. Abu let out a happy screech and the pair began to chase each other around the balcony.

Watching them play, Aladdin smiled. His plan had worked. He had made things right. But his smile faltered as he turned back toward where Jasmine stood with her father. Well, he had made *almost* everything right.

The Sultan caught his gaze and slowly walked over. Aladdin braced himself, ready to be reprimanded for his lies. But to his surprise, the Sultan reached out his hand. "How can I ever thank you?" he asked.

Aladdin felt his cheeks flush at the unexpected words. "You don't need to thank me," he said. "But will you at least accept my apology? I'm sorry that I lied to you both. But"—he stopped and turned to Jasmine—"especially to you. You deserve so much more."

The Sultan put a sympathetic hand on Aladdin's shoulder. "We are just men . . . we *all* make mistakes."

Feeling Jasmine's gaze on him, Aladdin shifted uncomfortably on his feet. The Sultan may have accepted his apology, but he still felt ashamed. Lowering his head, he went to stand by the Genie.

"Cheer up, Al," the Genie said. He had clearly forgiven Aladdin for his part in the terrible mess. "We can make this right. Last wish. Royalty was the right idea, so we should riff on that. Here's what I'm thinking . . ." He stopped and put a finger to his chin. "Aladdin, warrior prince, a noble heart in a land where thieves run feral. You like it?" He waited to see Aladdin's reaction. When he didn't move, the Genie shrugged and pressed on. "Last wish, come on. Back up, back up, Genie gonna give it to ya."

Aladdin nodded. He had thought long and hard about his last wish. He wanted to wish for something real, something that would count. Something that would mean something. The wish was obvious. Looking up at the Genie, he smiled. "Then for my third wish . . ."

The Genie cracked his knuckles, getting ready to make it happen. "Going big this time . . . gonna do this for you . . ."

"I wish . . ."Aladdin began, "to set you free, Genie."

Chapter
Twenty-Two

"What did you say?"

Aladdin smiled as the Genie stopped mid–magic conjuring and looked over at him. His eyes were big, his blue skin shining. Before Aladdin could repeat himself, the magic of the wish took hold. There was a puff of smoke and then, just like that, the Genie became a normal man. No longer blue, no longer larger than life, he morphed into a man, and as he did so, the gold cuffs which had marked him as a genie for thousands of years fell from his wrists.

He was free.

"Ooh, ooh, something's happening," the Genie said as the reality of what Aladdin had done began to hit him. He looked at his friend. "Tell me to do something."

"Get me some jam," Aladdin said.

Genie let out a happy shout when the words didn't make him feel compelled to do—or get—anything. "Get your own yam jam!" he shouted, his obvious glee making Aladdin smile. The Genie grabbed Aladdin in a huge bear hug, lifting him up off his feet and swinging him around. "Thank you!" he said. Then, lowering him back down, his eyes grew serious. "No, really, thank you."

"No, Genie," Aladdin said, shaking his head. "Thank *you* for everything." He paused. "What will you do now?"

"I don't know," the Genie said after a moment. "All I ever wanted was the freedom to choose. I always wanted to travel, see the world." He stopped and looked over at Dalia. "And there's this certain handmaiden I'd love to travel the world with, if she'll have me." Shooting Aladdin another smile, the Genie turned and made his way over to Dalia.

Aladdin watched as the Genie's head dipped closer to Dalia's and he whispered something in her ear. The handmaiden let out a happy laugh, her eyes twinkling. Watching the pair, Aladdin smiled sadly. He had given up his chance for happiness, but even while the thought of a future without Jasmine hurt, he wouldn't have done it differently. Leaning down, he placed the lamp on the ground.

Abu, who had finally stopped playing with the carpet, leapt up onto his shoulder. "Come on, Abu, let's go home," he said softly.

Jasmine, too, was watching Dalia and the Genie with a mixture of happiness and jealousy. As the pair whispered into each other's ears, Jasmine felt tears sting her eyes. She had come so close to her own happiness and then come even closer to losing everything. Now she didn't know what to feel or what to do. Feeling a gentle hand on her arm, she turned and found her father looking at her.

"I'm sorry, my dear," he said, his voice deep with emotion.

"It's all right, Baba," Jasmine said. "You don't need to—"

Her father raised a hand, stopping her. "Please let me finish," he said. He took a deep breath. "All I have wanted for you was to be safe and happy. Never to feel pain as I did. You are my love, my pride, my universe. I feared losing you, like I lost your mother." The tears she had been holding back began to fall as she listened to her father's words, hearing, for the first time, all the things she had wanted to hear since her mother had died. The Sultan, his own eyes misty, went on. "I only saw my little girl who I wanted to protect, not the woman you have become. You have shown me great courage and strength as mine is fading. You are right. This is not the Agrabah your mother wanted. *You* are the future of Agrabah, a true leader." He stopped, pulling off the ring that had belonged to his father and his father's father before that—all former sultans. The ring that was more symbolic to Jasmine than any crown or throne. Slowly, he held it out to her. "You shall be the next sultan of Agrabah."

Jasmine stared down at the ring, her heart swelling with pride and love as she accepted the ring and all it meant. "Thank you, Baba, but my greatest honor will always be that I'm your daughter."

The Sultan nodded. Pulling her into a hug, he squeezed her tightly. For a long moment, daughter and father simply stood, enjoying the moment of peace after all they had been through. And yet, as they stood there, Jasmine couldn't help thinking there was someone else she desperately wanted to see. Someone else she wanted to share her news—and her future—with. As if reading her thoughts, the Sultan pulled back. "Go find him," he said.

Pulling their attention away from each other, Dalia and the Genie looked over. "Go . . . go," they urged.

Jasmine didn't need to be told again. She raced off, her feet pounding down the corridors and stairs. She burst into the palace courtyard. Frantically, she looked around, hoping to see Aladdin. But the garden was empty. She knew he was heading home, but he hadn't left that long before her. He couldn't have possibly gotten farther than the gate. The gate! Once more, Jasmine took off, only this time her feet carried her toward the main entrance.

Jasmine's eyes traveled over the many people coming in and out of Agrabah. Then she spotted them—Aladdin, Abu, and the carpet were just outside the gates. Aladdin was walking slowly, staring down at something in his hand. Quickly, Jasmine walked up and fell into step behind them. As she peered past his shoulder, Jasmine's heart nearly burst when she saw what Aladdin was holding in his hand—her hairpin. He had kept it this whole time.

Smiling, she got right up behind the trio. "Stop! Thief!" she said.

Instantly, Aladdin stopped. Whipping around, he spotted Jasmine. She was out of breath and her cheeks were flushed, but Aladdin was sure she had never looked more beautiful. "Am I in trouble?" he asked.

Jasmine nodded at the hairpin. "Only because you got caught," she said, her tone teasing.

"I didn't mean to keep it!" Aladdin said. But both he and Jasmine knew that wasn't the truth. Grabbing her, Aladdin pulled her closer. Their noses touched and then, ever so gently, he lowered his mouth to hers. And with that kiss, they finally stole each other's hearts—completely and utterly.

Up on the balcony, Genie watched his friend finally get the girl. The Sultan watched his daughter find her true love. Exchanging a look, both men smiled. With Jasmine as sultan, and Aladdin by her side, Agrabah's future was golden.

Epilogue —
Seven Years Later

"**B**ut where did the Genie go, Baba?"

Barro looked up at his father as the man finished his story and steered the boat into the harbor. The city beyond was vibrant and alive. The streets and market bustled. Ships came in and out, carrying rich silks and colorful fruits and vegetables. Docking the ship, the mariner didn't answer his son right away.

Lindy pressed him. "Did Princess Jasmine and Aladdin get married?"

Finally, the mariner looked over at his children. "Yes, yes, they got married in a splendid celebration that was open to all." He pointed to a golden carriage that was making its way along the docks. "No interest in who's riding inside?" he asked.

Barro shrugged. "Looks aren't everything, Baba," he said, getting off the boat and sitting down on the dock. It felt strange not to have the shifting of the boat beneath him and he reached out a hand to steady himself on dry land.

"Don't be so narrow-minded," Lindy agreed as she and her mother walked down the gangway and joined Barro.

Realizing his children were growing impatient, the mariner held up his hands. They had someplace to be very soon. "Okay, okay," he said, ready to finish his story. "So, the Genie set out to see the world with the woman he loved. But he did eventually return to Agrabah. And do you know what Aladdin said the first moment he saw him?"

"What, Baba?" both Barro and Lindy asked, leaning forward in anticipation.

"I told him, I've never had a friend like you," came another voice.

Whipping around, the children looked up to find Aladdin and Jasmine standing behind them. On Aladdin's shoulder, Abu sat, munching on an apple, looking exactly as he had seven years before in the Cave of Wonders — only a little plumper.

With a laugh, Aladdin stepped forward, throwing his arms around his friend. Barro and Lindy looked back and forth between their father and Aladdin and Jasmine, their mouths hanging open.

Finally, Barro shook his head. "That means," he said, looking at his father, "that *you're the Genie*?"

"And *you're* the handmaiden, Mama?" Lindy asked, her eyes wide. Then she looked at Jasmine. "And *you're* the princess?"

Dalia smiled at her daughter. "Actually, she's the sultan now."

Jasmine looked over at Dalia and the old friends exchanged a happy look. Leaning down, she drew to eye level with Lindy and Barro. "I am Jasmine," she said. "And your mother is my dearest friend." Then she stood back up and looked over at her other dear friend, the mariner. "I hope your arrival means you're accepting our offer?"

The mariner shrugged. "We're not the ones you have to convince."

"Ah, I see . . ." Aladdin said. This time he was the one to address the children. "How would you like to come and live with us?" He held up an old beat-up lamp and smiled mischievously. "Beats living in here."

The mariner shook his head. "No, thank you, seen more than enough of that thing." He turned to Lindy and Barro and raised an eyebrow. "Children?"

Reaching out, Barro took the lamp. He began to rub its side. When nothing happened, he looked disappointed. "It doesn't work," he said. "There's no genie in it."

The mariner took the lamp from his son. "You don't need a genie to make your wishes come true," he said. His voice was full of emotion as he looked at his son and then at his gathered friends and family.

"It's not fair."

Lindy's small voice was barely audible in the hustle and bustle of the dock. But the mariner heard it. Kneeling down, he placed two large hands on her tiny shoulders. "What's not fair?" he asked.

"You did everything for everyone else and never got any wishes for yourself," Lindy said sadly.

The mariner shook his head and pulled his sweet daughter in for a hug. How wrong she was. He had gotten everything he could have ever wished for—and more. "I've got my three little wishes right here," he said, pulling back and wiping away the tear that slid down Lindy's cheek. There was nothing more in the world he could want or need than what he had right in front of him.

Standing, the mariner turned and put an arm around Dalia. Then he watched as Jasmine gestured for them all to climb onto the carpet. Looking over, the mariner met Aladdin's gaze. He nodded. He would happily accept his friend's offer to live in Agrabah. How could he not? He had already traveled the world with his favorite people in the world. It had been his wish to find freedom and Aladdin's wish to find happiness with Jasmine. Their wishes had come true. So now, all that was left was to live happily ever after.